SNARK

Being a true history of the expedition that
discovered the Snark and the Jabberwock ...
and its tragic aftermath

DAVID ELLIOT
after **LEWIS CARROLL**

OTAGO

For Gillian

CONTENTS

PREFACE TO THE 42ND EDITION

GABRIEL CLUTCH was a thief and a liar but he was right about one thing.

He told me he had a great secret in his collection that would shake the literary world to its roots if it ever got out. Whenever I challenged him to provide proof he would smile that irritating smile of his, tap the side of his nose and change the subject.

When the matter arose on my last visit, however, I noticed his mean little eyes flit nervously to a strange-shaped box tucked away on a dark shelf in the corner of his library.

Gabriel Clutch died the very next day.

Some weeks later I searched the aisles of books at his estate auction until I found it: Lot 42: A bicorne hatbox, c. 19th century, badly water damaged.

It had been pushed to the back of an overloaded trestle and was all but hidden behind a stack of aged and bound volumes of *Punch*. The frayed twine that fastened the box had been untied and the lid hung askew, but whoever had peered inside was no doubt as disappointed as I was to find it appeared to contain nothing more than a mouldering old bicorne hat. Sliding my hand beneath the tattered headpiece, however, amply repaid my faith in Clutch's deviousness. Something had been wrapped and crammed into the bottom of the box. I surreptitiously removed my hand, quietly closed the lid and refastened the twine.

I sat in trepidation through the first 41 auction lots. I needn't have worried: none of the other collectors seemed interested and the bidding for Lot 42 was over quickly. I couldn't wait to get Clutch's secret home.

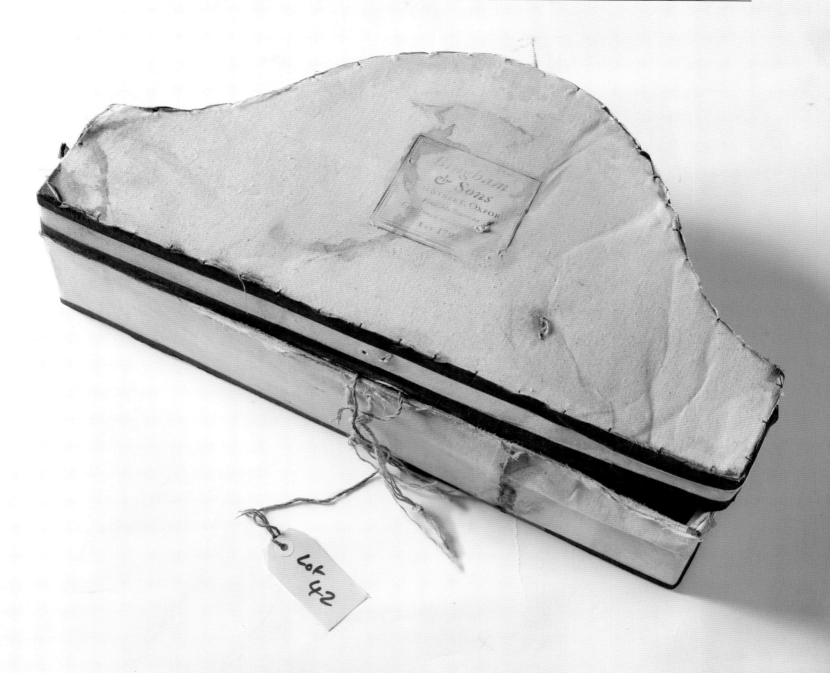

Thinking back now to that golden day, the whole episode seemed somehow radiant with my final victory over my rival. Once in my library I opened the curtains, cleared the clutter from my desk, and placed Clutch's battered box so that it caught the light streaming in through the window. The hat's faded braid glinted as I lifted it to one side and carefully eased the ragged bundle beneath from its hiding place. I had no inkling then of the darkness I was to uncover.

It was, as I suspected from its heft and dimensions, a book. I untied the musty cloth wrapping and revealed a stained, scarred, and in some places obviously gnawed cover that could barely contain its contents.

A veritable nest of pages filled with drawings and scribbled notes burst at all angles from its ruined binding, strangely filling my library with the scent of salt and adventure.

Afraid that it might disintegrate in a chaos of paper, I carefully lowered the journal, for journal it was, to my desk, put on a pair of felt gloves from my drawer and gently lifted the cover.

It was an extraordinary document. The copious notes and drawings by a character called 'the Boots', and in them he recorded a bizarre Victorian odyssey, an expedition of madmen in search of a fabled delicacy.

As I read on, I could not help but be caught up in the strangeness of the world they encountered. Yet there was a peculiar familiarity to it all, as if I had somehow travelled this road before. Above all was the nagging question of why Clutch had not had the book rebound and catalogued into his collection, had not treasured it and indeed crowed over its possession.

The afternoon slowly darkened into night and the salt smell that permeated the journal's pages gradually soured and sickened until my treasured library seemed to crowd down upon me in a jungle of shadows as I read. The Boots' story reeked of death and decay as the final tragic chapter played out.

I walked to my window, flung it open and breathed in the cool night breeze. I suddenly knew where I had read this story before … and I knew why Clutch had kept the journal secret.

He was afraid.

The fact was, this Boots' journal of his voyage and discoveries so closely resembled events described in certain famous works by Lewis Carroll that it couldn't possibly be coincidence. If it were true, it meant that Carroll's great poems, *The Hunting of the Snark* and *Jabberwocky*, were not mere fiction; rather, they related historical events. Although disguised in the ancient traditions of riddles and nonsense, these works had their origins in a real expedition to a real island. And 'the Boots' had been a member of that ill-fated expedition.

Somewhere in the darkness I could almost hear old Clutch laughing. He had turned the tables on me and his torment had become mine. Should I expose it to the world and be lauded for uncovering a sensational literary truth? Or, given the risk of utter humiliation if the journal were to be revealed as a fraud, should I return it to its hiding place and keep its secret to myself?

It has not been an easy decision.

For 20 years I have lived with the mystery of the Boots' notebook. In my many readings of his journal my fondness and admiration have grown for the courageous young man who created it and the ingenuity he displayed, often in conditions of extreme duress. He was naïve, perhaps, certainly foolhardy, but his observations and skill with a pen have left us with an invaluable record of a tragic expedition that I have come to believe most certainly took place. Furthermore, in making this record he has sounded a clear warning of an appalling predator that may yet survive in the wilderness of the ocean.

The Boots' sketches and notes must surely be the basis of many of the events later recounted by Lewis Carroll in *The Hunting of the Snark*; and that his record of one particularly mysterious incident was used by the poet as the inspiration for his famous *Jabberwocky* there can be no doubt.

How the great man came into possession of this journal, and how it eventually made its way into the hands of Clutch, remain a mystery, but I suspect Lewis Carroll might have found himself faced with the same dilemma as to its authenticity and its portent. His brilliant literary adaptations, cloaked as they are in nonsense, in a sort of portmanteau world between reality and fiction, are nonetheless redolent of dark forces at play.

When this book was first published 10 years ago I feared, as Clutch and perhaps even Carroll did, that my publication of the Boots' journal would be heaped with scorn by the literary establishment. Still, I felt a duty, for better or for worse, to bring this young man's story out into the light of day.

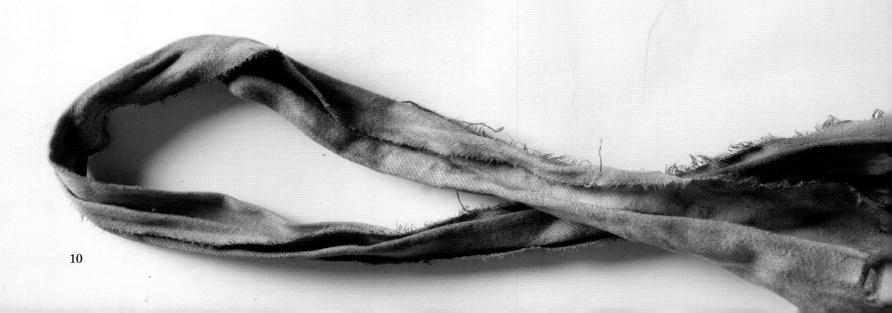

I realise I should have had more faith. There has been criticism—in fact outright derision from some quarters. Yet there has also been curiosity, and a willingness to cast aside preconceptions and examine the evidence with an unprejudiced eye.

In the time since the first printing I have received an avalanche of correspondence from readers wishing to know more about my research, more about certain incidents recorded by the Boots. Others have studied the journal drawings and notes and have written to me with their own comments. Many of these contributions bring clarity (of a sort) to the sometimes confusing narrative of the young adventurer as he struggles to make sense of the strange world in which he finds himself.

I have collated these contributions in the form of notes at the back of the book, in the order they are relevant to the story. I cannot guarantee, however, that premature reading of this information will not spoil some of the surprises the narrative offers. For those brave souls who wish to put themselves entirely in the hands of the Boots and his extraordinary story, these notes await you as an added delight at the end.

I hope that in the end you will believe, as I do, that the Boots' drawings and notes are testament that the island of the Snark exists. It waits for us out there somewhere, with its desolate chasms and crags, its dank, steaming tulgey wood, its surreal wildlife and perhaps, still brooding on its thwarted ambitions, that most devastating creature of all, the Boo—

But perhaps we should stop there. Perhaps it's time for the Boots to tell his own story and let you make up your own mind.

We begin, as the journal does, in Oxford about 1850.

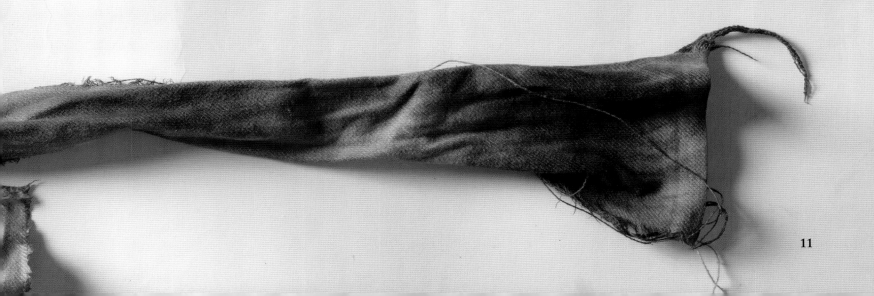

The Beginning

The Lecture

Hurrah! Fate has smiled upon me at last. This night, frustrated in my art and with little hope of enlightenment or entertainment, I attended a lecture entitled 'The Stomach Rules the World: The Gastronomy of Zoology'. Little did I suspect how the night would end.

When the lantern went out there was much loud patriotic discussion, a proposal put to the floor and a show of hands. And now I am enlisted in a great and noble enterprise! I am to be part of an expedition to obtain that most famous and elusive delicacy, the Snark. Our leader has ambitions to return with sufficient numbers to produce progeny and enrich the plates of England … and I shall be there to record it all for posterity.

We have all been given a list of things to acquire that we are assured will aid us in our venture, although I cannot readily see how. No doubt their use will become apparent.

I must make haste. We leave from Oxford Station at 9 a.m. Thursday.

My list
Tumblers
Forks
Soap
Railway share

Aardvak cuit à la
vapeur.

15

The Great Western Railway

Mr Brunel has produced a miracle of speed and noise! We head for Bristol at an astonishing pace. Sparks fly and smoke billows over our heads as we hurtle across the countryside. I can barely hold my pen to write.

In the first-class carriage ahead I can just make out the bicorne hat of our leader, the brave Bellman, as he leans out of the window, but the encouraging sound of his bell is lost in the general commotion. He is accompanied by his pet Beaver (rescued from a stew, I'm told). The rest of his crew appear to have been chosen to fulfil a range of occupations (none of them remotely nautical). I list them now: A maker of Bonnets and Hoods, A Barrister, A Broker, A Billiard-marker, A Banker, A Baker, A Butcher and myself (in third class), a humble Boots.

Bristol

Our ship is a fine vessel and rests at a jaunty angle on the beach. I am, however, a little concerned. It seems the Bellman is to be our captain and he insists he needs no guide to sail the ship other than his copy of the Naval Code (none of which he appears to understand).

It has taken us several hours to stow our goods aboard the vessel. Loaded at low tide when we were able to walk out to her, she now cannot right herself in the flood and remains stubbornly stuck to the sand under the waves. If we unload her and wait till she is floated, we ourselves sink and cannot walk out to her.

The large, wheeled contraption our leader assures us is essential for steeping a Snark has been loaded and unloaded several times, with increasing bitterness and recrimination. Our chickens, geese and pig now add their own protests to the general outcry, and the Bellman has taken to ringing his bell in a most agitated fashion.

At last a local fisherman has come to our aid, lightening our load by several boxes of provisions so that we may proceed to sea.

The Lighthouses

Wonderful news: I am to be the helmsman!

I am as yet a little unsure as to my duties but I gather they involve steering the ship and avoiding obstacles where possible. My main consideration under Rule 42 in our captain's copy of the Naval Code, however, is to strictly avoid any conversation with the rest of the crew. I suspect this is to avoid distraction from such an important responsibility.

This is the fourth day of our voyage and I fear we are making little progress. Our captain seems preoccupied with the appearance of the ship and becomes increasingly fastidious when we near the coast, which, I should point out, we have hardly left. This is particularly frustrating when we near a lighthouse, because he is continually ordering the unshipping and varnishing of various parts, particularly the bowsprit and the steering wheel, to 'catch the light', which leads to long delays whilst we wait for things to dry.

His instructions as to our course are confusing. The map he produced on Tuesday is of little help, having no information of use whatsoever.

Pig Overboard

Our continual hugging of the coastline has led to the most unfortunate loss of our pig. The sight and no doubt smell of land and freedom proved too much for the creature; while its enclosure was being dunged out it seized its chance, broke free of its bonds and threw itself over the side.

Our last sight was of its bobbing head as it struck out for the shore. I do not fancy its chances.

Phrenology

Three weeks have passed and we have at last made it out into the open sea. With the absence of lighthouses the need for varnishing seems to have diminished in the mind of our good captain and we have settled into our various shipboard routines. In my spare time I have sketched a plan of the ship and the places most often frequented by each of our crew. I am struck by how much it resembles one of Dr Gall's phrenology diagrams.

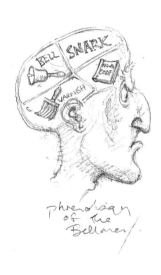

phrenology
of the
Bellman.

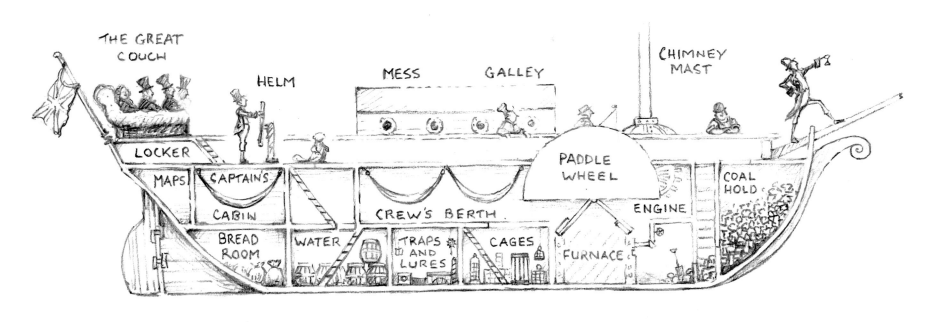

THE GREAT COUCH

HELM

MESS   GALLEY

CHIMNEY MAST

PADDLE WHEEL

LOCKER

MAPS

CAPTAIN'S CABIN

CREW'S BERTH

ENGINE

COAL HOLD

BREAD ROOM

WATER

TRAPS AND LURES

CAGES

FURNACE

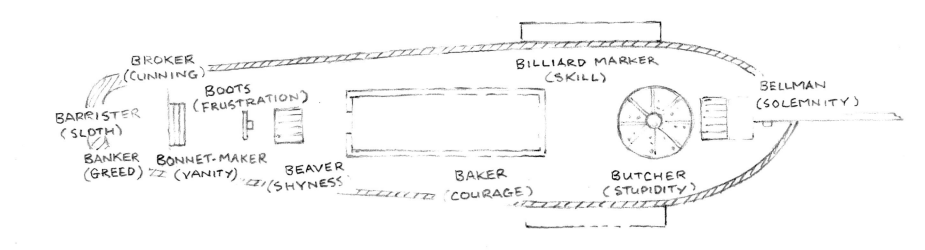

BROKER (CUNNING)

BARRISTER (SLOTH)

BANKER (GREED)

BONNET-MAKER (VANITY)

BOOTS (FRUSTRATION)

BEAVER (SHYNESS)

BAKER (COURAGE)

BILLIARD MARKER (SKILL)

BELLMAN (SOLEMNITY)

BUTCHER (STUPIDITY)

25

A Life on the Ocean Wave

A Gnawing Problem

There is little to do but watch the sea and I note there are signs of boredom among the crew. One of the more disturbing examples of this is the Beaver, who has begun chewing on various (sometimes essential) parts of the ship. To curtail this destructive behaviour the captain has come up with an ingenious distraction: lace-making.

It seems these creatures are very dexterous and almost as fond of using their hands as using their teeth. The lace the Beaver makes is fine and delicate and comprises tiny interlocked leaves that remind it, the Bellman thinks, of the willows of Saskatchewan. Being primarily nocturnal, however, the animal has poor eyesight. The Banker has very kindly offered the loan of his extra pair of glasses, although not without charging interest at the going rate of 10 per cent per annum.

Something in the Wind

The Baker is a generally affable fellow and nearly always passes with a friendly nod and a smile. He does, though, have rare moments when a black mood seems to descend upon him and he can be seen pacing the deck in an agitated fashion.

On one such an occasion recently he approached me and, cupping his hand to my ear whispered, 'Some are Boojums!', which I thought most peculiar. I judged it bad form to enquire further, however, for the next minute he was his old smiling self.

Of all the crew he spends the most time on deck taking the air. This preference for the outdoors is strange as he appears to feel the cold more than most, donning as he does an abundance of coats. He wears so many and of such a variety, in fact, that he disappears almost completely from view within them, and in a gale creates a veritable uproar of flapping cloth.

The Island

Our first sight of the island is at daybreak: a bleak wall of broken cliffs catching the early morning sun. Our captain is sure this is the place.

It seems to frown upon us with sharp, overhanging brows as we approach, but there is a breach in the cliffs that allows us passage.

I steer as well as I can: under the walls of rock, through a mouth of turbulent water and into the calm of a small circular bay beyond.

We drift in silence, each lost in his own thoughts, each hat on the head of my companions at its own peculiar angle, each mouth agape to its own individual degree.

The swallows perched and teetering here and there on the cliffs about us stare back, equally stupefied, until the silence is shattered by the rattle of the anchor chain, the wingbeats of a thousand birds taking flight, and the toll of the Bellman's bell.

THE HUNTING OF THE SNARK

BY
LEWIS CARROLL

Fit the First:

THE LANDING

'Just the place for a Snark!' the Bellman cried,
 As he landed his crew with care;
Supporting each man on the top of the tide
 By a finger entwined in his hair.

'Just the place for a Snark! I have said it twice:
 That alone should encourage the crew.
Just the place for a Snark! I have said it thrice:
 What I tell you three times is true.'

The crew was complete: it included a Boots—
 A maker of Bonnets and Hoods—
A Barrister, brought to arrange their disputes—
 And a Broker, to value their goods.

A Billiard-marker, whose skill was immense,
　　Might perhaps have won more than his share—
But a Banker, engaged at enormous expense,
　　Had the whole of their cash in his care.

There was also a Beaver, that paced on the deck,
　　Or would sit making lace in the bow:
And had often (the Bellman said) saved them from wreck,
　　Though none of the sailors knew how.

There was one who was famed for the number of things
　　He forgot when he entered the ship:
His umbrella, his watch, all his jewels and rings,
　　And the clothes he had bought for the trip.

He had forty-two boxes, all carefully packed,
　　With his name painted clearly on each:
But, since he omitted to mention the fact,
　　They were all left behind on the beach.

The loss of his clothes hardly mattered, because
　　He had seven coats on when he came,
With three pair of boots—but the worst of it was,
　　He had wholly forgotten his name.

He would answer to 'Hi!' or to any loud cry,
　　Such as 'Fry me!' or 'Fritter my wig!'
To 'What-you-may-call-um!' or 'What-was-his-name!'
　　But especially 'Thing-um-a-jig!'

While, for those who preferred a more forcible word,
　　He had different names from these:
His intimate friends called him 'Candle-ends',
　　And his enemies 'Toasted-cheese'.

'His form is ungainly—his intellect small—'
　　(So the Bellman would often remark)
'But his courage is perfect! And that, after all,
　　Is the thing that one needs with a Snark.'

He would joke with hyænas, returning their stare
　　With an impudent wag of the head:
And he once went a walk, paw-in-paw, with a bear,
　　'Just to keep up its spirits,' he said.

He came as a Baker: but owned, when too late—
　　And it drove the poor Bellman half-mad—
He could only bake Bride-cake—for which, I may state,
　　No materials were to be had.

The last of the crew needs especial remark,
    Though he looked an incredible dunce:
He had just one idea—but, that one being 'Snark',
    The good Bellman engaged him at once.

He came as a Butcher: but gravely declared,
    When the ship had been sailing a week,
He could only kill Beavers. The Bellman looked scared,
    And was almost too frightened to speak:

But at length he explained, in a tremulous tone,
    There was only one Beaver on board;
And that was a tame one he had of his own,
    Whose death would be deeply deplored.

The Beaver, who happened to hear the remark,
    Protested, with tears in its eyes,
That not even the rapture of hunting the Snark
    Could atone for that dismal surprise!

It strongly advised that the Butcher should be
    Conveyed in a separate ship:
But the Bellman declared that would never agree
    With the plans he had made for the trip:

Navigation was always a difficult art,
    Though with only one ship and one bell:
And he feared he must really decline, for his part,
    Undertaking another as well.

The Beaver's best course was, no doubt, to procure
    A second-hand dagger-proof coat—
So the Baker advised it—and next, to insure
    Its life in some Office of note:

This the Banker suggested, and offered for hire
    (On moderate terms), or for sale,
Two excellent Policies, one Against Fire,
    And one Against Damage From Hail.

Yet still, ever after that sorrowful day,
    Whenever the Butcher was by,
The Beaver kept looking the opposite way,
    And appeared unaccountably shy.

Fit the Second:

THE BELLMAN'S SPEECH

The Bellman himself they all praised to the skies—
  Such a carriage, such ease and such grace!
Such solemnity, too! One could see he was wise,
  The moment one looked in his face!

He had bought a large map representing the sea,
  Without the least vestige of land:
And the crew were much pleased when they found it to be
  A map they could all understand.

'What's the good of Mercator's North Poles and Equators,
　　Tropics, Zones, and Meridian Lines?'
So the Bellman would cry: and the crew would reply
　　'They are merely conventional signs!

'Other maps are such shapes, with their islands and capes!
　　But we've got our brave Captain to thank'
(So the crew would protest) 'that he's bought *us* the best—
　　A perfect and absolute blank!'

This was charming, no doubt; but they shortly found out
　　That the Captain they trusted so well
Had only one notion for crossing the ocean,
　　And that was to tingle his bell.

He was thoughtful and grave—but the orders he gave
　　Were enough to bewilder a crew.
When he cried 'Steer to starboard, but keep her head larboard!'
　　What on earth was the helmsman to do?

Then the bowsprit got mixed with the rudder sometimes:
　　A thing, as the Bellman remarked,
That frequently happens in tropical climes,
　　When a vessel is, so to speak, 'snarked'.

But the principal failing occurred in the sailing,
　　And the Bellman, perplexed and distressed,
Said he *had* hoped, at least, when the wind blew due East,
　　That the ship would *not* travel due West!

But the danger was past—they had landed at last,
　　With their boxes, portmanteaus, and bags:
Yet at first sight the crew were not pleased with the view,
　　Which consisted of chasms and crags.

The Bellman perceived that their spirits were low,
　　And repeated in musical tone
Some jokes he had kept for a season of woe—
　　But the crew would do nothing but groan.

He served out some grog with a liberal hand,
    And bade them sit down on the beach:
And they could not but own that their Captain looked grand,
    As he stood and delivered his speech.

'Friends, Romans, and countrymen, lend me your ears!'
    (They were all of them fond of quotations:
So they drank to his health, and they gave him three cheers,
    While he served out additional rations.)

'We have sailed many months, we have sailed many weeks,
    (Four weeks to the month you may mark),
But never as yet ('tis your Captain who speaks)
    Have we caught the least glimpse of a Snark!

'We have sailed many weeks, we have sailed many days,
    (Seven days to the week I allow),
But a Snark, on the which we might lovingly gaze,
    We have never beheld till now!

'Come, listen, my men, while I tell you again
    The five unmistakable marks
By which you may know, wheresoever you go,
    The warranted genuine Snarks.

'Let us take them in order. The first is the taste,
    Which is meagre and hollow, but crisp:
Like a coat that is rather too tight in the waist,
    With a flavour of Will-o'-the-wisp.

'Its habit of getting up late you'll agree
    That it carries too far, when I say
That it frequently breakfasts at five-o'clock tea,
    And dines on the following day.

'The third is its slowness in taking a jest.
    Should you happen to venture on one,
It will sigh like a thing that is deeply distressed:
    And it always looks grave at a pun.

'The fourth is its fondness for bathing-machines,
    Which it constantly carries about,
And believes that they add to the beauty of scenes—
    A sentiment open to doubt.

'The fifth is ambition. It next will be right
    To describe each particular batch:
Distinguishing those that have feathers, and bite,
    From those that have whiskers, and scratch.

'For, although common Snarks do no manner of harm,
    Yet, I feel it my duty to say,
Some are Boojums—' The Bellman broke off in alarm,
    For the Baker had fainted away.

Fit the Third:

THE BAKER'S TALE

They roused him with muffins—they roused him with ice—
    They roused him with mustard and cress—
They roused him with jam and judicious advice—
    They set him conundrums to guess.

When at length he sat up and was able to speak,
    His sad story he offered to tell;
And the Bellman cried 'Silence! Not even a shriek!'
    And excitedly tingled his bell.

There was silence supreme! Not a shriek, not a scream,
    Scarcely even a howl or a groan,
As the man they called 'Ho!' told his story of woe
    In an antediluvian tone.

The Baker revives.

'My father and mother were honest, though poor—'
     'Skip all that!' cried the Bellman in haste.
'If it once becomes dark, there's no chance of a Snark—
     We have hardly a minute to waste!'

'I skip forty years,' said the Baker, in tears,
     'And proceed without further remark
To the day when you took me aboard of your ship
     To help you in hunting the Snark.

'A dear uncle of mine (after whom I was named)
     Remarked, when I bade him farewell—'
'Oh, skip your dear uncle!' the Bellman exclaimed,
     As he angrily tingled his bell.

'He remarked to me then,' said that mildest of men,
     '"If your Snark be a Snark, that is right:
Fetch it home by all means—you may serve it with greens,
     And it's handy for striking a light.

'"You may seek it with thimbles—and seek it with care;
     You may hunt it with forks and hope;
You may threaten its life with a railway-share;
     You may charm it with smiles and soap—"'

('That's exactly the method,' the Bellman bold
     In a hasty parenthesis cried,
'That's exactly the way I have always been told
     That the capture of Snarks should be tried!')

'But oh, beamish nephew, beware of the day,
     If your Snark be a Boojum! For then
You will softly and suddenly vanish away,
     And never be met with again!'

'It is this, it is this that oppresses my soul,
　　When I think of my uncle's last words:
And my heart is like nothing so much as a bowl
　　Brimming over with quivering curds!

'It is this, it is this—' 'We have had that before!'
　　The Bellman indignantly said.
And the Baker replied 'Let me say it once more.
　　It is this, it is this that I dread!

'I engage with the Snark—every night after dark—
　　In a dreamy delirious fight:
I serve it with greens in those shadowy scenes,
　　And I use it for striking a light:

'But if ever I meet with a Boojum, that day,
　　In a moment (of this I am sure),
I shall softly and suddenly vanish away—
　　And the notion I cannot endure!'

Fit the Fourth:
THE HUNTING

The Bellman looked uffish, and wrinkled his brow.
    'If only you'd spoken before!
It's excessively awkward to mention it now,
    With the Snark, so to speak, at the door!

'We should all of us grieve, as you well may believe,
    If you never were met with again—
But surely, my man, when the voyage began,
    You might have suggested it then?

'It's excessively awkward to mention it now—
    As I think I've already remarked.'
And the man they called 'Hi!' replied, with a sigh,
    'I informed you the day we embarked.

'You may charge me with murder—or want of sense—
    (We are all of us weak at times):
But the slightest approach to a false pretence
    Was never among my crimes!

'I said it in Hebrew—I said it in Dutch—
    I said it in German and Greek:
But I wholly forgot (and it vexes me much)
    That English is what you speak!'

''Tis a pitiful tale,' said the Bellman, whose face
    Had grown longer at every word:
'But, now that you've stated the whole of your case,
    More debate would be simply absurd.

'The rest of my speech' (he explained to his men)
    'You shall hear when I've leisure to speak it.
But the Snark is at hand, let me tell you again!
    'Tis your glorious duty to seek it!'

'To seek it with thimbles, to seek it with care;
  To pursue it with forks and hope;
To threaten its life with a railway-share;
  To charm it with smiles and soap!

'For the Snark's a peculiar creature, that won't
  Be caught in a commonplace way.
Do all that you know, and try all that you don't:
  Not a chance must be wasted to-day!

'For England expects—I forbear to proceed:
  'Tis a maxim tremendous, but trite:
And you'd best be unpacking the things that you need
  To rig yourselves out for the fight.'

Then the Banker endorsed a blank check (which he crossed),
    And changed his loose silver for notes.
The Baker with care combed his whiskers and hair,
    And shook the dust out of his coats.

The Boots and the Broker were sharpening a spade—
    Each working the grindstone in turn:
But the Beaver went on making lace, and displayed
    No interest in the concern:

Though the Barrister tried to appeal to its pride,
    And vainly proceeded to cite
A number of cases, in which making laces
    Had been proved an infringement of right.

The maker of Bonnets ferociously planned
    A novel arrangement of bows:
While the Billiard-marker with quivering hand
    Was chalking the tip of his nose.

But the Butcher turned nervous, and dressed himself fine,
    With yellow kid gloves and a ruff—
Said he felt it exactly like going to dine,
    Which the Bellman declared was all 'stuff'.

'Introduce me, now there's a good fellow,' he said,
    'If we happen to meet it together!'
And the Bellman, sagaciously nodding his head,
    Said 'That must depend on the weather.'

The Beaver went simply galumphing about,
    At seeing the Butcher so shy:
And even the Baker, though stupid and stout,
    Made an effort to wink with one eye.

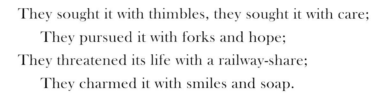

Fit the Fifth:

THE BEAVER'S LESSON

They sought it with thimbles, they sought it with care;
　　They pursued it with forks and hope;
They threatened its life with a railway-share;
　　They charmed it with smiles and soap.

Then the Butcher contrived an ingenious plan
　　For making a separate sally;
And had fixed on a spot unfrequented by man,
　　A dismal and desolate valley.

But the very same plan to the Beaver occurred:
　　It had chosen the very same place:
Yet neither betrayed, by a sign or a word,
　　The disgust that appeared in his face.

Each thought he was thinking of nothing but 'Snark'
　　And the glorious work of the day;
And each tried to pretend that he did not remark
　　That the other was going that way.

But the valley grew narrow and narrower still,
      And the evening got darker and colder,
Till (merely from nervousness, not from good will)
      They marched along shoulder to shoulder.

Then a scream, shrill and high, rent the shuddering sky,
      And they knew that some danger was near:
The Beaver turned pale to the tip of its tail,
      And even the Butcher felt queer.

He thought of his childhood, left far far behind—
      That blissful and innocent state—
The sound so exactly recalled to his mind
      A pencil that squeaks on a slate!

''Tis the voice of the Jubjub!' he suddenly cried.
      (This man, that they used to call 'Dunce'.)
'As the Bellman would tell you,' he added with pride,
      'I have uttered that sentiment once.

''Tis the note of the Jubjub! Keep count, I entreat;
      You will find I have told it you twice.
'Tis the song of the Jubjub! The proof is complete,
      If only I've stated it thrice.'

The Beaver had counted with scrupulous care,
      Attending to every word:
But it fairly lost heart, and outgrabe in despair,
      When the third repetition occurred.

It felt that, in spite of all possible pains,
    It had somehow contrived to lose count,
And the only thing now was to rack its poor brains
    By reckoning up the amount.

'Two added to one—if that could but be done,'
    It said, 'with one's fingers and thumbs!'
Recollecting with tears how, in earlier years,
    It had taken no pains with its sums.

'The thing can be done,' said the Butcher, 'I think.
    The thing must be done, I am sure.
The thing shall be done! Bring me paper and ink,
    The best there is time to procure.'

The Beaver brought paper, portfolio, pens,
    And ink in unfailing supplies:
While strange creepy creatures came out of their dens,
    And watched them with wondering eyes.

So engrossed was the Butcher, he heeded them not,
    As he wrote with a pen in each hand,
And explained all the while in a popular style
    Which the Beaver could well understand.

'Taking Three as the subject to reason about—
　　A convenient number to state—
We add Seven, and Ten, and then multiply out
　　By One Thousand diminished by Eight.

'The result we proceed to divide, as you see,
　　By Nine Hundred and Ninety and Two:
Then subtract Seventeen, and the answer must be
　　Exactly and perfectly true.

'The method employed I would gladly explain,
 While I have it so clear in my head,
If I had but the time and you had but the brain—
 But much yet remains to be said.

'In one moment I've seen what has hitherto been
 Enveloped in absolute mystery,
And without extra charge I will give you at large
 A Lesson in Natural History.'

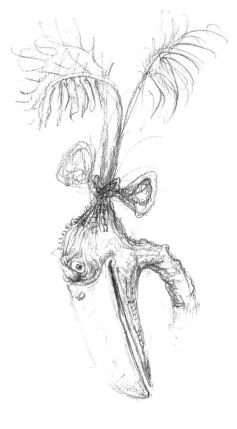

In his genial way he proceeded to say
     (Forgetting all laws of propriety,
And that giving instruction, without introduction,
     Would have caused quite a thrill in Society),

'As to temper the Jubjub's a desperate bird,
     Since it lives in perpetual passion:
Its taste in costume is entirely absurd—
     It is ages ahead of the fashion:

'But it knows any friend it has met once before:
     It never will look at a bribe:
And in charity-meetings it stands at the door,
     And collects—though it does not subscribe.

'Its flavour when cooked is more exquisite far
     Than mutton, or oysters, or eggs:
(Some think it keeps best in an ivory jar,
     And some, in mahogany kegs:)

'You boil it in sawdust: you salt it in glue:
     You condense it with locusts and tape:
Still keeping one principal object in view—
     To preserve its symmetrical shape.'

The Butcher would gladly have talked till next day,
     But he felt that the Lesson must end,
And he wept with delight in attempting to say
     He considered the Beaver his friend.

While the Beaver confessed, with affectionate looks
     More eloquent even than tears,
It had learned in ten minutes far more than all books
     Would have taught it in seventy years.

They returned hand-in-hand, and the Bellman, unmanned
    (For a moment) with noble emotion,
Said 'This amply repays all the wearisome days
    We have spent on the billowy ocean!'

Such friends, as the Beaver and Butcher became,
    Have seldom if ever been known;
In winter or summer, 'twas always the same—
    You could never meet either alone.

And when quarrels arose—as one frequently finds
    Quarrels will, spite of every endeavour—
The song of the Jubjub recurred to their minds,
    And cemented their friendship for ever!

THE BARRISTER'S DREAM

They sought it with thimbles, they sought it with care;
    They pursued it with forks and hope;
They threatened its life with a railway-share;
    They charmed it with smiles and soap.

But the Barrister, weary of proving in vain
    That the Beaver's lace-making was wrong,
Fell asleep, and in dreams saw the creature quite plain
    That his fancy had dwelt on so long.

He dreamed that he stood in a shadowy Court,
    Where the Snark, with a glass in its eye,
Dressed in gown, bands, and wig, was defending a pig
    On the charge of deserting its sty.

The Witnesses proved, without error or flaw,
    That the sty was deserted when found:
And the Judge kept explaining the state of the law
    In a soft under-current of sound.

The indictment had never been clearly expressed,
    And it seemed that the Snark had begun,
And had spoken three hours, before any one guessed
    What the pig was supposed to have done.

The Jury had each formed a different view
    (Long before the indictment was read),
And they all spoke at once, so that none of them knew
    One word that the others had said.

'You must know—' said the Judge: but the Snark exclaimed, 'Fudge!
    That statute is obsolete quite!
Let me tell you, my friends, the whole question depends
    On an ancient manorial right.

'In the matter of Treason the pig would appear
    To have aided, but scarcely abetted:
While the charge of Insolvency fails, it is clear,
    If you grant the plea "never indebted".

'The fact of Desertion I will not dispute;
    But its guilt, as I trust, is removed
(So far as relates to the costs of this suit)
    By the Alibi which has been proved.

'My poor client's fate now depends on your votes.'
    Here the speaker sat down in his place,
And directed the Judge to refer to his notes
    And briefly to sum up the case.

But the Judge said he never had summed up before;
    So the Snark undertook it instead,
And summed it so well that it came to far more
    Than the Witnesses ever had said!

When the verdict was called for, the Jury declined,
    As the word was so puzzling to spell;
But they ventured to hope that the Snark wouldn't mind
    Undertaking that duty as well.

So the Snark found the verdict, although, as it owned,
    It was spent with the toils of the day:
When it said the word 'GUILTY!' the Jury all groaned,
    And some of them fainted away.

Then the Snark pronounced sentence, the Judge being quite
    Too nervous to utter a word:
When it rose to its feet, there was silence like night,
    And the fall of a pin might be heard.

'Transportation for life' was the sentence it gave,
    'And *then* to be fined forty pound.'
The Jury all cheered, though the Judge said he feared
    That the phrase was not legally sound.

But their wild exultation was suddenly checked
    When the jailer informed them, with tears,
Such a sentence would have not the slightest effect,
    As the pig had been dead for some years.

The Judge left the Court, looking deeply disgusted:
    But the Snark, though a little aghast,
As the lawyer to whom the defence was intrusted,
    Went bellowing on to the last.

Thus the Barrister dreamed, while the bellowing seemed
    To grow every moment more clear:
Till he woke to the knell of a furious bell,
    Which the Bellman rang close at his ear.

Fit the Seventh:

THE BANKER'S FATE

They sought it with thimbles, they sought it with care;
    They pursued it with forks and hope;
They threatened its life with a railway-share;
    They charmed it with smiles and soap.

And the Banker, inspired with a courage so new
    It was matter for general remark,
Rushed madly ahead and was lost to their view
    In his zeal to discover the Snark.

But while he was seeking with thimbles and care,
    A Bandersnatch swiftly drew nigh
And grabbed at the Banker, who shrieked in despair,
    For he knew it was useless to fly.

He offered large discount—he offered a cheque
    (Drawn 'to bearer') for seven-pounds-ten:
But the Bandersnatch merely extended its neck
    And grabbed at the Banker again.

Without rest or pause—while those frumious jaws
　　Went savagely snapping around—
He skipped and he hopped, and he floundered and flopped,
　　Till fainting he fell to the ground.

The Bandersnatch fled as the others appeared:
　　Led on by that fear-stricken yell:
And the Bellman remarked, 'It is just as I feared!'
　　And solemnly tolled on his bell.

He was black in the face, and they scarcely could trace
    The least likeness to what he had been:
While so great was his fright that his waistcoat turned white—
    A wonderful thing to be seen!

To the horror of all who were present that day,
    He uprose in full evening dress,
And with senseless grimaces endeavoured to say
    What his tongue could no longer express.

Down he sank in a chair—ran his hands through his hair—
    And chanted in mimsiest tones
Words whose utter inanity proved his insanity,
    While he rattled a couple of bones.

'Leave him here to his fate—it is getting so late!'
    The Bellman exclaimed in a fright.
'We have lost half the day. Any further delay,
    And we shan't catch a Snark before night!'

Fit the Eighth:
THE VANISHING

They sought it with thimbles, they sought it with care;
 They pursued it with forks and hope;
They threatened its life with a railway-share;
 They charmed it with smiles and soap.

They shuddered to think that the chase might fail,
 And the Beaver, excited at last,
Went bounding along on the tip of its tail,
 For the daylight was nearly past.

'There is Thingumbob shouting!' the Bellman said.
 'He is shouting like mad, only hark!
He is waving his hands, he is wagging his head,
 He has certainly found a Snark!'

They gazed in delight, while the Butcher exclaimed
　　'He was always a desperate wag!'
They beheld him—their Baker—their hero unnamed—
　　On the top of a neighbouring crag,

Erect and sublime, for one moment of time.
　　In the next, that wild figure they saw
(As if stung by a spasm) plunge into a chasm,
　　While they waited and listened in awe.

'It's a Snark!' was the sound that first came to their ears,
　　And seemed almost too good to be true.
Then followed a torrent of laughter and cheers:
　　Then the ominous words 'It's a Boo- '

Then, silence. Some fancied they heard in the air
    A weary and wandering sigh
That sounded like '-jum!' but the others declare
    It was only a breeze that went by.

They hunted till darkness came on, but they found
    Not a button, or feather, or mark,
By which they could tell that they stood on the ground
    Where the Baker had met with the Snark.

In the midst of the word he was trying to say,
    In the midst of his laughter and glee,
He had softly and suddenly vanished away—
    For the Snark *was* a Boojum, you see.

THE END

Dawn and Despair

It rained during the night and the chill air carried a dank fog in from the sea. In an effort to keep warm we have stoked the Snark-cooker with driftwood and it smoulders on the beach, adding to the miasma with vile, sour smoke.

My companions continue to sleep around me, the variety of their snores mingling with the soft lapping of the waves. The peacefulness of the scene belies the strange and tragic episodes of our previous night. As I poke the fire I notice that several strange little snails have clustered around the embers for warmth.

I am sure none of the others has the heart to continue the hunt.

For myself, I cannot believe that the poor Baker has disappeared so utterly. From the top of the bluff last night I thought I could make out, in the dying light, a patch of vegetation in the centre of the island. Perhaps there is hope yet that he may have fallen and, dazed and disorientated, wandered in that direction.

I resolve on my course. I must make one last effort to find my friend the Baker. I gather a few provisions—some bread, a little cheese and a lantern—and leave my crewmates a note of my intentions.

Inland

After climbing over bluffs and trudging through valleys for what seems an
age, I find myself again at the scene of the tragedy. Below me, the chasm that
seemed to swallow the Baker lies in deep shadow. Somewhere far off I hear
again the shriek of the bizarre bird we encountered on the hunt. I glance
constantly back over my shoulder for reassuring signs of smoke from our
encampment, but I have come too far.

I do my best to shake off my misgivings, turn again to my quest and
reach into my bag for my sketchbook.

From this, one of the highest points on the island, I draw a simple map
of my surroundings. As I follow the coastline with my pencil I am struck by
how closely the island resembles a creature curled up on the surface of the sea.

Caught up like a whirlpool in the very centre is the area of vegetation I
saw the night before. I am resolved to begin my search there.

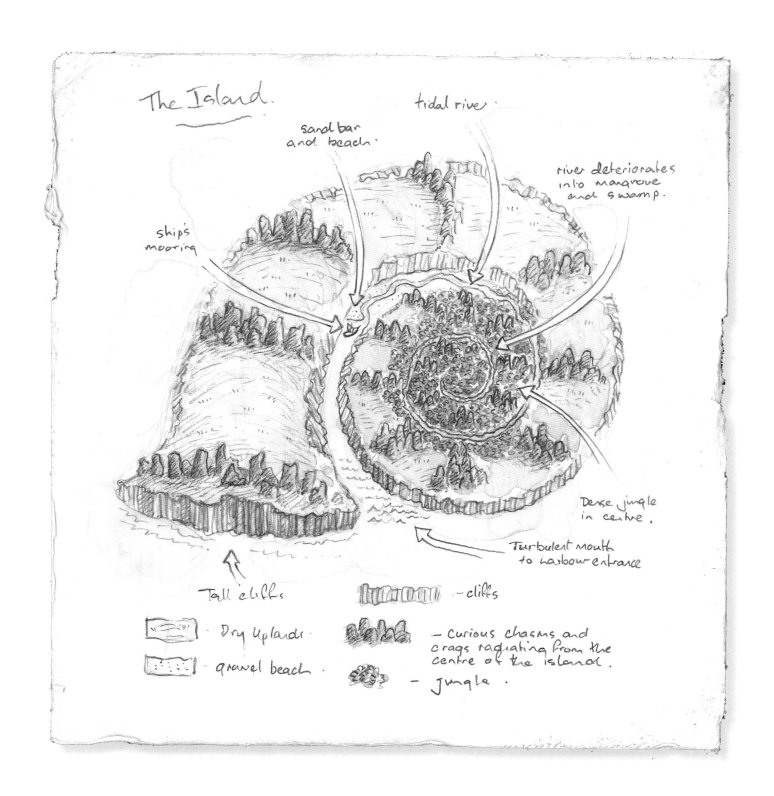

The Island.

tidal rive

sand bar
and beach.

river deteriorates
into mangrove
and swamp.

ship's
mooring

Dense jungle
in centre.

Turbulent mouth
to harbour entrance

Tall cliffs

- cliffs

- Dry Uplands

- Curious chasms and
crags radiating from the
centre of the island.

- gravel beach

- Jungle.

The Tulgey Wood

As I descend, the sparse scrubby cover among the rocks gradually transforms itself into ever denser and greener forest. Soon I find myself in a lush jungle-like world of twisting vines and huge buttressed trees, many of which I suspect are unknown to science. The air is suddenly hot and thick with exotic scents from huge flowers that drape pendulously from the branches above. Strange animal and bird cries fill my ears. I call out for the Baker and the forest falls silent momentarily—then the cries resume, if anything, louder than before.

More disturbing is the distant sound of trees splintering and falling in the path of what I tell myself is just some large herbivore browsing. My search of the undergrowth for signs of my friend's passing reveals strange clawed tracks of alarming size and disturbing gashes sliced into the bark of trees. There are more crashing sounds, this time a little closer, although it is difficult to tell from quite where.

I am beset by the suspicion that something might be following my trail, and keep a wary eye on the forest behind me.

Then, in a moment my fears are forgotten. There is a break in the canopy above and beams of sunlight burst down as if sent to illuminate the wonders of this astonishing forest. I stand in a botanist's paradise. Some plants tremble at my approach, sending forth showers of pollen that float in the air like small golden clouds. Others have rows of tooth-like spines and give off a sour and rancid odour. One most peculiar tree has a stout and wrinkled trunk of an incongruous light pink hue and sprouts

*branches with hand–like appendages that point accusingly into the shadows of
the surrounding forest.*

*I give up trying to make sense of it all, merely collecting and recording
what I can.*

*A glance at my pocket–watch warns me that the day is slipping away. I am
about to abandon my search, to turn and leave this place, when I hear cries and
whimpers of such piercing sadness I cannot resist seeking their origin.*

I fight my way through the undergrowth …

The Wabe

I am quite unprepared for the scene that suddenly unfolds before me.

Prising myself out from between two huge palm fronds, I find myself in a grand garden—or at least the sad and overgrown remnants of what must once have been a grand garden.

Dishevelled hedges struggle across what is less a clearing now than a hole in the surrounding forest. Thick vines snake down from the trees and wind across mouldering flowerbeds, intent on strangling lines of ancient rose bushes. Grasses and brambles erupt everywhere through broken stone paths.

In what appears to be the centre there is a small grassy mound studded with an unruly collection of sundials. They tilt and lean at a confusion of angles, at odds with one another over the correct hour. Between them lie heaps of weathered sticks.

In the very middle of this peculiar arrangement crouch the source of the plaintive cries. Six pigs wail in unison, regarding me with small, suspicious, tear-filled eyes.

Sharing their grief are some ragged parrot-like birds perched disconsolately at intervals among the stone plinths.

Careful not to disturb what I am sure are unrecorded species, I lower myself onto a stone step and quietly retrieve my sketchbook from my bag. The creatures, perhaps reassured that I mean no harm, resume their lamentations while I draw.

The cause of their anguish appears to be several badger-like creatures. As I watch, they leap about, frantically scratching the earth and showering their protesting victims with soil. From time to time, these strangely tufted mustelids break off to frolic and roll about on the slopes with seeming glee at the distress they are causing.

The Tower

I am quite lost in my drawing when I have the uneasy feeling that I am being watched. Then I notice my subjects are staring at something beyond their hill and out of my view.

Replacing my book in my bag, I creep deeper into the garden. There I am confronted with an astonishing structure. Beyond the garden and rising above the trees, its curving, spiralling walls catching the last of the afternoon sun, is a huge tower. It is as if some grand pavilion has gone through a sort of metamorphosis, its columns, arches and domes broken into bits, then twisted and woven with great beams of timber into something altogether more organic and sinister—something almost alive.

Here and there incongruous details protrude: the prow of a man-of-war, an equestrian statue, a garden fork, an advertising poster for soap and the rear end of a bathing-machine.

Around the base curls an evil-looking ditch of stagnant green water. The tower appears to float above it, absorbed in its own macabre reflection. A rotting wooden bridge slides under a mouldering archway into darkness.

Dwarfed in its shadow, I am so preoccupied with recording the tower in my journal that I am unaware of the great danger I am in. If it weren't for the curious whiffling noise the creature's tail makes as it stalks up behind me I would have no warning and, I'm quite certain, would not be here to tell the tale. As it is, I just manage to leap to one side as the beast lunges, its great claws slicing through thin air where my head was but a moment before. In that instant I see it: the blazing eyes, gaping jaws full of teeth, dagger-like talons on each of its strange long legs …

And that is enough. I run. Before the beast can charge again I run—to the only place that seems to offer any hope of refuge at all. I run across the bridge, under the archway and into the darkness of the great tower.

All I can think of is to escape those flaming eyes, those terrible jaws and claws. I run headlong into blackness until I trip and sprawl across the sodden floor. Then I crawl until I can crawl no further and huddle against the farthest wall.

The fearsome frame of the beast fills the entrance and I flinch from the shadows of its talons as they grope towards me in my hiding place. The whole tower shakes to the beast's frustrated roars and bellows but for some reason it comes no further.

There I stay until at long last the massive creature shakes its great head and, with one last elephantine rumble of anger, departs.

I continue to crouch in the gloom, straining my ears for any sound of its return.

Gradually, as my heart stops pounding, I start to become aware of the utter change in my situation. It is as if I have stepped over not just the threshold of the tower but the boundary between one world and another. The sound of wind rustling in the trees is now drowned by the relentless booming of an unseen ocean, the pungent scents of fruits and flowers overwhelmed by the reek of seaweed, salt and decay. This is surely no place of the forest—as different to the domain of the beast outside as night is to day—and I begin perhaps to understand the creature's reluctance to enter.

It occurs to me that in my surprise at discovering this place and my frantic dash to find safety within its walls I have given no thought to the reasons behind its strange appearance—or indeed what might have built it. Now I wonder what new horror awaits me in the shadows.

Summoning my courage I take my lantern from my bag, light the wick and, holding it before me, creep forward into the unknown.

The tower is hollowed out into one vast, empty, damp space that compresses into darkness above me in a sweeping spiral which—were it not so oppressive—would be almost beautiful. Slime-covered walls appear in my lantern light as I turn in a slow circle.

I breathe a sigh of relief. I am spared for the moment. There is nothing here but dripping walls and sodden rubble … but weighing more heavily upon me each moment is my suspicion that my sanctuary brings with it new, undiscovered dangers.

I confess I am bitterly regretting my rash decision to leave my sleeping companions on the beach and mount my lone search for the Baker. Whatever threats, real or imagined, surround me, my only safety now is with the crew back on our vessel. Pulling my bag onto my back I return to the entrance and peer out across the bridge; my plan is to dash to the cover of the trees before I am detected.

But one look at the ruined garden tells me I have left it too late. Night has fallen and the dark arms of the forest have closed around the clearing in an impenetrable barrier. I am trapped.

I have no option but to use the tower as my shelter overnight and hasten back to the ship at break of day. I can only pray that I will remain alone and undisturbed.

I make myself as comfortable as I can in the cheering light of my little lamp, eat the last of my bread and cheese and drink some water. As my eyes are now accustomed to the gloom, I venture to explore the perimeter of my prison, seeking some clues to its history.

I have not gone far before my lantern entices a dull reflection from something half buried in the rubble. Scraping with a shard of stone, I gradually unearth a most curious object. It is, I am almost certain, a military bugle, but so bent, twisted and inexplicably studded with shells it is almost unrecognisable. Most perplexing of all are the delicate wings attached to either side of its bell tube.

I fumble for my notebook and place my lantern on the floor so my hands are free to sketch, but there is something in the mystery and dark import of the bewildering instrument that stays my hand almost as soon as I have begun. My bag is already quite full and I must discard a number of my precious samples to make room but I determine to retrieve the bugle to the ship for further study.

My attention is drawn to a faint glow in the wall nearby, where a curtain of slime has sloughed away. Pulling off more strands of the dripping sludge, I am surprised to find that the surface beneath has a strange, layered, milky appearance.

It shimmers with iridescent pearl-like pools that seem to well up to meet the glow from my lamp. At first their liquid shapes seem to dance and flow to the pounding of the phantom sea, but gradually, deep within its substance, vague forms take shape and begin to move, as if my lantern were somehow awakening a world entombed within the wall. Small, sharp shapes appear and scuttle between languid fronds. As I watch, entranced, these slowly dissolve and re-form into crag-like silhouettes against a spectral landscape, and the sound of the ocean is silenced by the distant, now familiar scream of the maniac bird lost somewhere in the haze within the wall.

I must work fast if I am to sketch the astonishing transformations taking place before me. By now the crags have also vanished and in their stead a dense forest sways to a wind that seems to emanate from within the wall itself. The trees gradually part before me and I am confronted with a scene that is at once new and strangely familiar.

Paths snake through the shadows on the wall and I recognise the hill from the ruined garden outside, although it has but one single sundial and its creatures meander contentedly on the well-tended lawn. Beyond the hill, in what must be the very spot on which I now stand, I can make out the silhouette of what appears to be a pavilion, and indeed I perceive the turret that has been so brutally absorbed into the strange edifice that now towers above me.

Is this some sort of dream I am witnessing? Or a memory, perhaps, captured in the milky layers of the wall? A memory of the island, this garden, in a happier, more civilised time, when nature was to some degree tamed and the terrors of the wild held at bay?

My reverie is broken by first sniffles, then cries, then wails coming from the wall. The creatures of the sundial hill appear to be cowering on the lawn in some distress. Something is about to happen … I reach for my pencil in the hope that I may render the shifting scenes before they disappear.

JABBERWOCKY

BY
LEWIS CARROLL

(from *Through the Looking-Glass and What Alice Found There*, 1872)

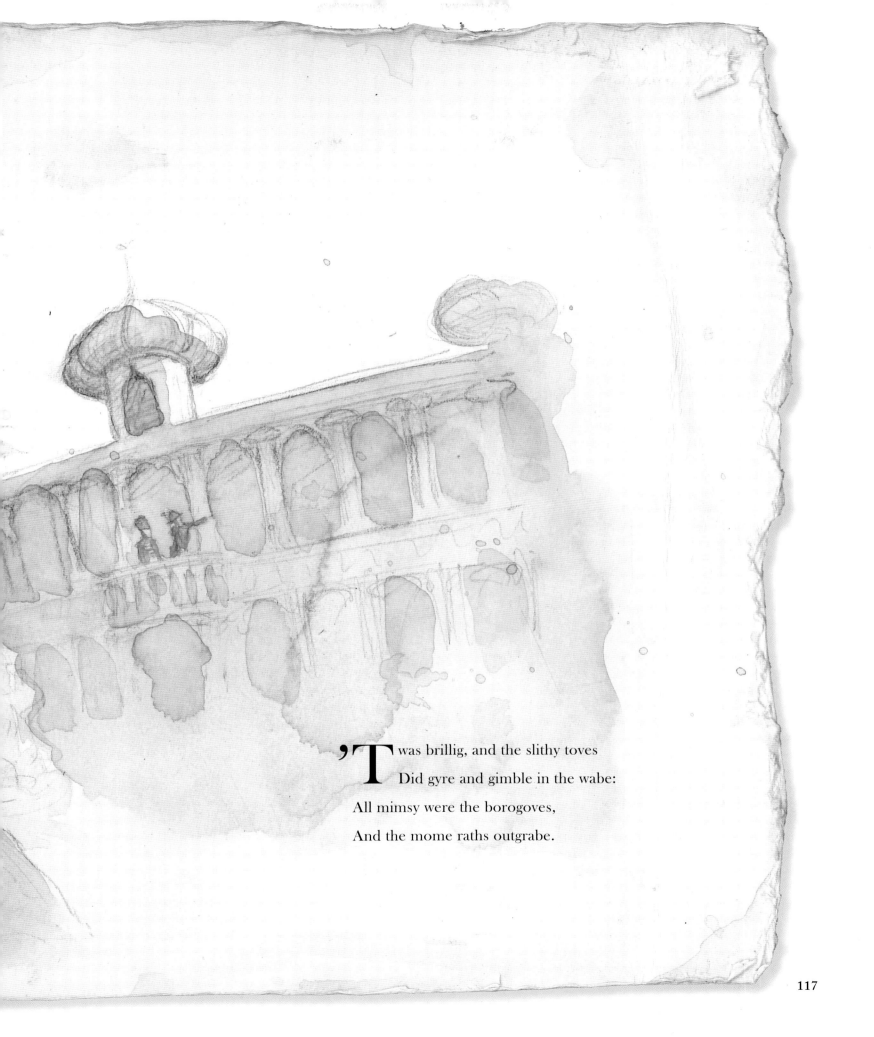

'Twas brillig, and the slithy toves
Did gyre and gimble in the wabe:
All mimsy were the borogoves,
And the mome raths outgrabe.

'Beware the Jabberwock, my son!
The jaws that bite, the claws that catch!
Beware the Jubjub bird, and shun
The frumious Bandersnatch!'

He took his vorpal sword in hand:

Long time the manxome foe he sought —

So rested he by the Tumtum tree,
And stood awhile in thought.

124

And, as in uffish thought he stood,
The Jabberwock, with eyes of flame,
Came whiffling through the tulgey wood,
And burbled as it came!

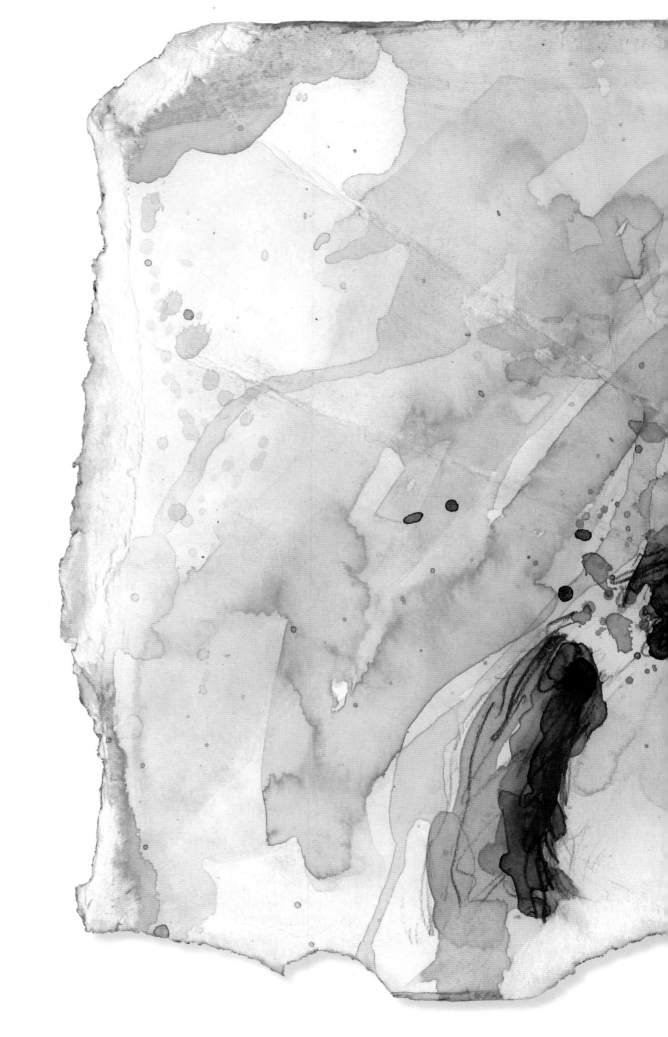

126

One, two! One, two! And through and through
The vorpal blade went snicker-snack!

He left it dead, and with its head
He went galumphing back.

128

'And hast thou slain the Jabberwock?
    Come to my arms, my beamish boy!
O frabjous day! Callooh! Callay!'
    He chortled in his joy.

'Twas brillig, and the slithy toves
    Did gyre and gimble in the wabe;
All mimsy were the borogoves,
    And the mome raths outgrabe.

Beast

My lantern begins to gutter and the wall grows dim and lifeless in the
waning light. I slump exhausted to the floor and rub my tired eyes, trying
to remember the jumble of scenes I have just witnessed. My notebook is
ripped and my frenzied attempts to keep pace with the mysterious images
lie scattered all around me. Collecting up the pages, I attempt to sort them
into some sort of order, and despair when I see that my drawings are
crude, and stained and blotted in my haste.

I find the garden and the turreted pavilion—the soldier as he is given
his mission—his ride forth on his hunt … I shudder when I recognise that
his quarry is the very same kind of creature that attacked me so recently—
and almost cheer when the beast is despatched so bravely. But my smile
quickly fades when I remember that the noble building the huntsman
returns to so triumphantly is now transformed into this horrific tower.
Furthermore, there is no sign of these civilised men other than
their ethereal shadows in the wall, and their garden has begun to
revert to the wild. Worse still, one of the beasts they hunted still roams
the surrounding forest and no doubt lies in wait for me at this very
moment. Some powerful and evil force is at work here but I am too
exhausted to think further.

My lantern flickers for the last time and my world plunges into darkness.

135

I cannot sleep and huddle shivering, rubbing my arms and hands against the chill and damp. The dawn when it finally comes is thin and frail and seems to linger around the entrance to the tower as if afraid of what it might find. I gather my things, stow the bugle carefully in my bag and hazard a few steps out into the growing light.

A massive bite has been taken out of the bridge and the earth on the far bank has been torn up and trampled by the beast in its frustrated rampage. Can I dare hope that the creature has exhausted itself, that it is asleep, that it does not keep watch?

The animals of the sundial hill stand silently and observe me with wide, staring eyes as I creep past. I have nearly reached the far end of the garden when one of the pigs, perhaps overcome by the palpable tension in the air, bursts into noisy tears. Others rush to comfort it, but too late. A great rumbling bellow erupts from the forest and a flock of shrieking birds lifts from the trees. Branches snap and the earth trembles. I must run for my life.

Nothing can compare to the terror I know in that headlong dash
through the forest.

My one slim advantage is my size. As I leap through gaps in the trees,
dodge branches and swing across gullies, the lumbering beast, from the
sound of the splintering jungle behind me, seems content simply to smash
through all obstacles to get at me. Nevertheless I am losing ground with
each snagging thorn, each clinging vine, each slip and stumble.

As I reach the rocks and rising scrubland at the edge of the forest I
stand and turn, my chest heaving. Below I can clearly see the trail of
destruction wrought by the beast, cutting a straight line towards me.
I have no time to rest. I turn and begin climbing with all the speed I can
muster but it seems any edge I might have had is now lost in this tortured
landscape of chasms and crags. Where I scrabble and slide on the crumbling
slopes the beast merely leaps from bluff to bluff on its long legs.

I glimpse the dark shape bounding towards me across the broken horizon. I dare not raise my head for fear of detection as I scuttle through the maze of ravines in a deadly game of cat and mouse. The beast is so close now I can sometimes hear its breath. Its murderous shadow looms behind boulders and clefts as it stalks through the corridors of rock. It is only a matter of time until it will be on me.

Then suddenly I hear a wonderful sound: the faint but unmistakeable crash of waves on the beach. Hope begins to rise in my chest. If I can hear the sea perhaps my crewmates might be able to hear me. I will raise the alarm, let them know of my predicament, and surely they will come.

The bugle! I had almost forgotten it. Will it still work? It is a faint hope, I know, but all I have.

Judging that it might be more effective from some height, I edge my way up a nearby crag. As I reach the summit I look down to see the beast crouching in the chasm below me, its muzzle in the very crevice I have just vacated.

I ease the bugle from my bag, lift it to my lips and blow with all my might.

A blast of sound bursts out across the broken landscape, leaping and rebounding from rock and stone, cliff and cave, bluff and scarp—away, away into the distant valleys—then back it comes, my one small bugle multiplied a hundredfold, resounding louder and louder in a deafening crescendo.

Below, the startled beast runs first this way then that in its confusion, red eyes blazing, talons splayed. Faced with what it must think is a cavalry charge of foes, it lopes away into the ravines, burbling as it goes.

I am overjoyed at my reprieve and make haste in the direction of the sea. At any moment I hope to meet my crewmates rushing to my rescue, but when I finally reach the heights above the beach I see they are still ensconced aboard the ship.

I shout and wave from the cliff-top and they call back but I cannot tell if theirs are cries of greeting or impatience.

Then I hear a snarl behind me—and I know they are cries of warning.

The beast's eyes move slowly from my face to my hand still holding the bugle and back again—I can feel its fury at how it has been deceived.

It crouches, and then with a roar suddenly springs and we are both falling through the air.

The beast's jaws are nearly about my throat when the impact of the ground breaks me loose from its grasp. I somersault and tumble down the sliding shingle, the beast just behind me, snapping its terrible teeth and raking the air with its talons as it tries to reach me across the avalanche of stones.

In the split second it takes the cumbersome creature to get to its feet I am already sprinting towards the surf. My crewmates yell encouragement as I dash headlong into the waves and strike out towards the ship.

Each second I expect to be seized and dragged back ashore in the beast's jaws but my terror has given me strength I could never have hoped for. As hands reach down to haul me aboard our ship I look back to see the beast flinging up great showers of sand on the beach, and I hear the bay echoing with its bellows of frustrated rage.

145

146

Escape

The crew have no time for my stories and thrust me towards the tiller, while the Bellman impatiently rings his bell for the anchor to be weighed.

Is it just my imagination? Are the cliffs above leering out and threatening to hurl great rocks down upon us? Does the island crouch and make as if to leap and gather us back into its stone claws as we struggle to unfurl our sail and escape?

As we reach the harbour mouth we hear one last, lingering, bone-chilling scream from the cliffs above.

For once our craft obeys the tiller and we make it safely to the open sea. The crew, as one, give a hearty cheer. Hats are thrown in the air and men embrace as comrades.

I would join in, I too would cheer with all my might, but for the captain sternly ringing his bell to remind me that under Rule 42 of the Naval Code I must avoid conversation with the rest of the crew.

Still, it is with a lighter heart that I stand at the wheel and watch that cursed island dipping below the horizon astern.

Great Expectations

We have been at sea now for a week. My ordeal must have taken its toll for I have not had the energy to keep up my notes and have several times fallen asleep at the wheel.

There is only one thought on our minds now, and that is the sceptred isle we call Home.

I'm sad to say a general air of pompous self-congratulation has begun to prevail. The loss of the poor Baker seems forgotten as each of my fellow crew members, reclining languidly on the Great Couch, reflects more and more generously on his own heroic role in the adventure.

I overhear talk of the anticipated reception on our return—the bunting, the cheers, the adoring crowds, and how each might, when pressed (and much against his modest nature), recount how he faced the Snark and triumphed.

I'm not sure how plausible our story will sound without a single specimen to show for our efforts.

Perhaps we could show them the snails that have somehow made their way on board. They seem to be everywhere. If I didn't know better I would think they were listening to the conversation.

Snails

I must say the snails are beginning to become a problem.

Yesterday the Barrister found one wearing his wig, and this morning the Banker discovered another inside his cashbox grazing on five-pound notes. The Bellman often has to shake one or two out of his bell before he can commence ringing.

At first the crew were well disposed towards our little stowaways and indeed tried to befriend them as pets. Unfortunately, try as they might, they found them unwilling to engage in any interaction. I had a little more success when I brought out the bugle, which appeared to have them most intrigued.

Burial at Sea

We have sailed for three weeks under a good breeze and fair skies but our wind and good fortune have now deserted us. Despite the Bellman's furious ringing, we are becalmed.

Two more days and still no wind. Everyone is becoming a little terse and short-tempered. The Bellman has, at last, rung for the boiler to be stoked and sent the Beaver below to the coal hold.

It has been some hours now and the Beaver has not returned. The crew has been searching.

It is now a full day since the Beaver disappeared and we must consider it lost. A small service was held and the Bellman (with tears in his eyes, for it was his Beaver) dropped some of the animal's delicate lace creations over the side. We all sang 'God Save The Queen'.
Suspicion has fallen on the Butcher.

Disturbingly, our search for the Beaver revealed even more snails, some of such large proportions they quite crowd out the gangways.

Suicide?

Yesterday, strangely, one of the ship's ventilation funnels was found unbolted amidships and decorated with an assortment of bows. The Bonnet-maker denies all responsibility.

The wind has picked up again and we have been making good headway all week.

I am sad to say the Butcher disappeared yesterday. The general consensus is that, overcome with remorse for murdering the Beaver, he has thrown himself overboard. The Barrister says it is a justice of sorts.

The crew is now actively gathering up the snails and tipping them into the sea.

Another week and now we have lost both the Broker and the Billiard-marker. A fearful silence has fallen over the ship, except that the Bellman is ringing his bell with a new urgency over the stern of the ship to make it go faster.

Storm

Rough weather with a rising gale and we barely have enough men to bring in the sail. The Bonnet-maker and the Banker are gone. The Banker's cashbox and the Bellman's hatbox slide together endlessly up and down the deck, to the surge of the swell. No one is bothered to pick them up.

The Bellman's tinkling grows weaker. I cannot look him in the face.

The Barrister went first. I think I heard the beginning of an objection— but perhaps it was a gull crying in the distance.

Then the Bellman's bell gave one last, mournful toll and was heard no more.

I am the last.

There is just the endless ocean, the roar of the wind in the sail and the strange little snails that now seem to cling to every rail and rope of the ship.

How could it have come to this?

Revelations

I am overwhelmed by a great sense of loneliness and the certainty that I will be next; that my own meeting with oblivion is just a matter of time. My only companions are the snails and I notice that a small, feathered example has climbed to the top of the ship's wheel before me. What enigmatic little creatures they are.

In search of comfort, perhaps, I reach out to stroke the animal's feathers but withdraw my hand with a cry as I feel a sharp pain and glimpse a row of sharp teeth vanishing beneath the creature's shell. In my shock I lash out, sending the snail spinning from the wheel. It clatters across the deck and comes to rest with a feathery squeak against a railing.

Suddenly a deathly hush seems to fall over the ship. I feel as if I am being watched by a thousand eyes. I become aware that I am now completely surrounded by a living carpet of snails. More begin pouring out of portholes, streaming from ventilation shafts and dropping from the rigging.

Soon they are crowding around me, nudging at my boots, trying to gain purchase on the leather. I kick them away but they return in ever-greater numbers, clambering over one another in their determination to get to me. I am hemmed in by rocking, clacking shells. Trapped against the wheel, I look about desperately for some sort of sanctuary and notice a strange commotion a few feet away, near the Great Couch. A folder spilling what look like railway-shares is sliding across the deck, driving before it tumbling armies of retreating snails.

Lashing out left and right, I manage to retrieve the folder. In desperation I arm myself with a fistful of the shares and turn to flourish them at the snails.

'Back!' I yell, and back they go, rippling and rattling across the deck in a living wave. But I must be vigilant to keep them at bay.

Why the shares threaten them so I have no idea, but my mind returns to the peculiar list of equipment given to me at the beginning of our voyage: soap, thimbles ... and most pertinently, it now seems, the railway-shares!

A terrible thought suddenly strikes me. Could it be so simple and so horribly ironic? Could it be that our quarry has been under our noses all the time? That the very creatures we sought were all about us as we searched blindly among the chasms and crags, faced maniac birds and savage beasts ... as we lost our dear Baker? Are these snails in fact Snarks?

To test my theory I take one of the small silver thimbles that remain in my pocket and toss it into the throng of shells. Immediately there is a great scrabbling and clattering as the snails surge about the thimble in a frenzied whirlpool of desire. There is no longer any doubt in my mind. These hundreds, these thousands of snails are SNARKS ...

I throw another thimble, causing another snail stampede, this time towards the galley. While they are distracted I spread some of the railway-shares in a defensive circle around my wheel. Then I slump down, trying to think clearly about my predicament.

The fact that some of these creatures bite, and seem able to act en masse ... These are frightening developments. Could it be that the creatures we have hunted are in fact hunting us? Is it possible that hordes of Snarks could overwhelm and administer a death of a thousand tiny bites—like some sort of land piranha? Yet when I think of attacking piranha I think of screaming and blood, not the silent, empty disappearances that have plagued our expedition.

The Snarks have closed in again, jostling eagerly in a circle some feet from my railway-share fortress, all signs of their former belligerence gone. I toss a third thimble and watch them tumble over each other in eager pursuit. No, these little creatures could not be responsible for our wholesale elimination: they are too fickle, too simple, too easily distracted from their purpose. It would need something bigger and more powerful, something far, far worse.

162

Boojum

At that very moment I hear a great cracking and splintering of timbers and feel the ship shudder and slew in the water. The deck over the coal hold splits asunder and a huge dark form rises slowly from the gaping hole, its massive weight crushing a deep agonised groan from the ship's wooden hull. With its huge spiral shell festooned with pillaged pieces of our vessel, it is undoubtedly another Snark, but of unbelievable proportions.

And there, as if to confirm my worst fears, like some macabre growth on its sliding black surface, is the laughing figure of the Baker, his finger extended. I watch in horror as my friend, frozen forever in his gesture of discovery, disappears over the curve of the still growing shell, and I remember his whispered warning, so long ago:

'Some are BOOJUMS!'

Boojum! The word now seems too trivial, a mockery, like the Baker himself, a small comic mask fastened to the face of an enormous terror.

Transfixed at my wheel, I watch the sections of shell as they rise before me, my eyes searching for any signs of my other lost companions. I see none but I am in no doubt that this creature, this Boojum, is responsible for their murders and will surely account for mine.

166

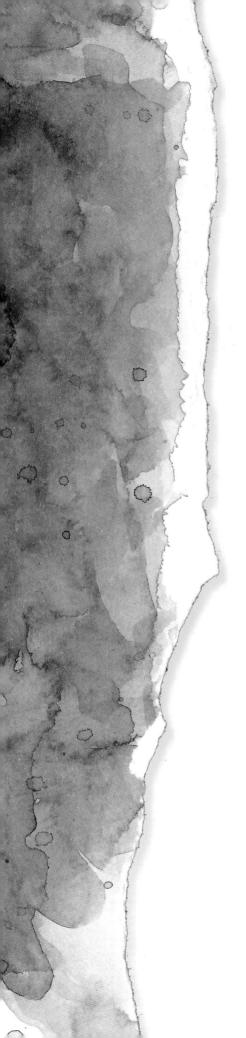

It would seem we are all destined to become mere ornaments, trophies displayed on the walls of a giant gastropod. The irony of this fate would be laughable were it not so appalling.

My hands drop to my sides and I await my fate.

The great shell looms over me like a huge, armour-plated serpent about to uncoil. But to my astonishment I remain unharmed. The sounds of the sea, the wind, the waves are suffocated under a dreadful silence. All I can hear is my heart pounding as I grasp the wheel once more.

Metamorphosis

The Boojum grows larger and larger each day.

The ship groans as if in pain as the beast continues to feast upon it, the decking beneath my feet reverberating to the splintering of timbers and the grinding of metal plates.

The little Snarks have now lost all interest in me and crawl over the great coil like infants in a mother's caress. They nestle among the collection of found and refashioned items that constitute the bizarre scales and spines growing from the giant creature's shell. Our Snark-cooker has been devoured, digested and regurgitated; so too our funnel, mast, paddle wheels, exhausts and pistons. Our useless sails have reappeared as the canvas roof and walls of a funereal bathing-machine.

My suspicions of the Boojum's murderous work on our return voyage are confirmed when I recognise the Beaver's tail hanging, and a set of the Butcher's knives protruding (neatly, in order of size) from the crest of its shell.

It is strange to relate that the horror of my situation—and the mystery of my continued survival—have dissipated somewhat in the routine and tedium of my days. Each sunrise I think might be my last, but then the next comes and I am still here. The voyage continues unhindered; indeed, the growing shell appears to be acting as a larger and larger sail, catching the trade winds and carrying us along at an increasing rate of knots. It seems that as long as I remain at the helm I am tolerated, in fact ignored.

spiral!

cavity.

cavity.

spiral!

cavity!

cavity

spiral.

Furtively I begin to revisit my journal in an attempt to unravel the mystery of these creatures. As I thumb through its early pages I now notice that Snark after Snark (or snail after snail, as I thought), each with its own peculiarly ornamented shell, appears almost unbidden in the margins of my drawings. It is almost as if they have been trying to attract my attention.

Examining the sketches of my journey through the ruined garden I arrive once more before the bizarre tower with its incongruous mass of swirling timber and carved stone. I gaze at my hurried attempts to capture the darkness of its cavernous interior until my eyes light on the strange bugle with its spiralling tubes and perplexing wings … and at last the mist clears from my eyes. I suddenly see the obvious underlying theme—of spirals and cavities—in shell, bugle and tower. They are but the same phenomenon at different orders of magnitude, a pattern replicated and enlarged exponentially. The Boojum has inhabited all these spiral cavities in turn—and is now on board my ship …

The wind has changed direction and I must put my hands to the wheel. There is a terrible rending and groaning of timber as the Boojum twists itself to a tacking angle. It seems determined to maintain our present course.

Night descends. The ship is now riding very low and heavily in the water yet still we sail on, a nightmare on the sleeping sea.

Nemesis

Dawn comes and with it the first flocks of seabirds I have seen since we left the island. My heart should lift at this promise of land, but if anything it plummets deeper into despair.

I have spent a sleepless night going over and over the tragedy of our expedition and thinking further on the nature of our nemesis, the Boojum. The equestrian statue on the creature's tower I now realise was the entombed body of the horseman I saw riding across its walls, frozen in his moment of triumph in much the same way as my friend the Baker. I cannot begin to understand what perverted digestive process is involved, but it seems the beast is not only capable of absorbing the flesh of its victims but somehow also captures images and episodes from their lives in the swirling lenses of its shell. I try not to think, as I write, about how the lives of my crewmates might be perpetually depicted inside the gargantuan form towering above me. Do the Baker's coats flap in a never-ending gale? Does the little Beaver galumph on an endless circuit of the walls? Does the Bellman's bell ring on interminably in the darkness?

But this is not the worst of it. It is the Boojum's actions since we arrived on its island that fill me with disquiet. What was its motive in abandoning its tower, hijacking the hunt and contriving to stow away on our ship? I fear there can only be one reason. It has its murderous appetite turned towards my beloved England, and I am being used to bring it to its prize.

Another sleepless night. As the dawn light catches on the crest of the towering behemoth above me, then gradually floods down over the jostling groups of little Snarks gathered in its spiralling folds, I ponder again the link between the two: the massive and the minuscule.

Reaching into my bag, I take out the mysterious bugle and cradle it in my lap. I feel again the sense of dark import amd foreboding I did when I found it in the tower. I am convinced that this twisted, reeking mass of dinted metal, feathers and shells, innocently snarkish but simultaneously imbued with menace, is the pivot on which our fortune has turned. Was this man-made artefact shining with martial glamour the instrument of our demise, seducing one of the little shelled creatures from its snarkish path and setting it on the road to becoming a Boojum? Was it thus the intervention of man that distorted the natural order? Did we bring this dreadful fate upon ourselves?

The bugle is uninhabited now. I have no idea what it looked like—the creature that squirmed and plotted within its convoluted tubes. Yet it seems to me there is no better specimen of Snark, caught here between its innocent beginning and its monstrous conclusion.

Perhaps there is one last duty I can perform for our doomed expedition. As I take out my pencil and begin to draw, I imagine the ghosts of my entombed crewmates gathered around to watch over my shoulder.

At last our hunt is at an end.

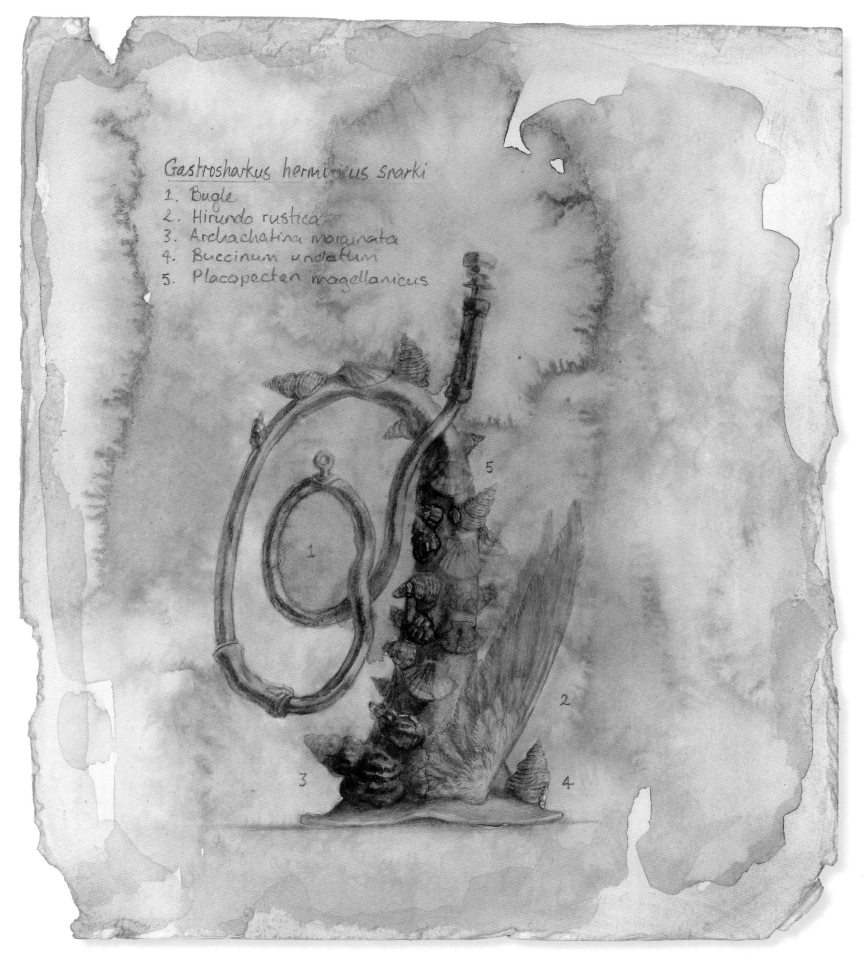

Gastrosharkus hermiticus snarki

1. Bugle
2. *Hirundo rustica*
3. *Archachatina marginata*
4. *Buccinum undatum*
5. *Placopecten magellanicus*

Beloved Land

Night is falling just as the dark edge of a coastline appears over our bow.
The Boojum has now grown to such a size that there is little left of
the ship except our rudder cutting a white line through the dark water.
We are like a great black wheel rolling inexorably across the sea.

179

The beam of a lighthouse suddenly splits the darkening sky and my worst fears are realised. Smeaton's Tower stands oak-like against the surf, England at its back. I am home.

Snarks, gathered in barnacle-like clumps on the foremost edge of the Boojum, seem to jostle one another in eager anticipation.

I go about my preparations unobserved. The rope to jam the rudder is tied in place as the Snarks begin to show alarm at the growing roar of the breakers.

We will go onto the rocks together.

My last small hope is to jump just before the impact.

My precious notes and drawings I am stowing in the Bellman's hatbox. They are the only legacy of our great expedition. If you find them, please take them back to Oxford. Let the good people there know for what we strove: for adventure, for knowledge, for Empire.

And let them know why we failed.

For the Snark was a Boojum, you see.

Notes

Notes to the 42nd Edition

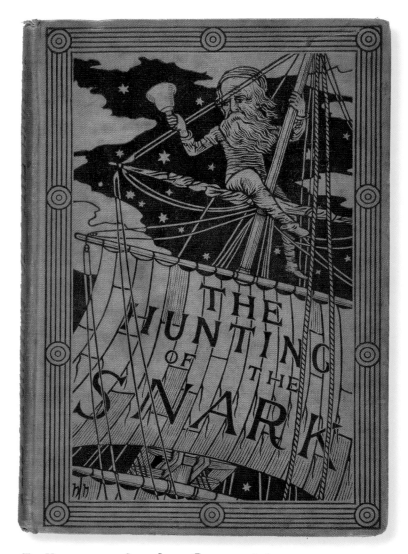

The Hunting of the Snark, Lewis Carroll, 1876

As stated in the introduction, since the book's first printing (and its subsequent unparalleled success through 41 editions) I have been inundated with correspondence from readers wishing to share their opinions, interpretations and (in some cases) undoubted expertise with regard to the Boots' journal and the expedition in general. To these I have added the fruits of my own research over the last 20 years.

As you will read, there remain many unanswered questions and intriguing lines of enquiry ripe for further investigation. Perhaps there are those among you who will take up the challenge.

However, it is probably helpful to begin first by presenting Carroll's Preface to his parody of the expedition, *The Hunting of the Snark*, as it refers (albeit sardonically) to several of the events and facts recorded by the Boots.

The most important of these is the connection between the search for the Snark and the discovery of the predator Carroll calls the Jabberwock.

THE MAN AT THE HELM

PREFACE TO *THE HUNTING OF THE SNARK*

If—and the thing is wildly possible—the charge of writing nonsense were ever brought against the author of this brief but instructive poem, it would be based, I feel convinced, on the line (in Fit the Second): *Then the bowsprit got mixed with the rudder sometimes.*

In view of this painful possibility, I will not (as I might) appeal indignantly to my other writings as a proof that I am incapable of such a deed: I will not (as I might) point to the strong moral purpose of this poem itself, to the arithmetical principles so cautiously inculcated in it, or to its noble teachings in Natural History—I will take the more prosaic course of simply explaining how it happened.

The Bellman, who was almost morbidly sensitive about appearances, used to have the bowsprit unshipped once or twice a week to be revarnished, and it more than once happened, when the time came for replacing it, that no one on board could remember which end of the ship it belonged to. They knew it

was not of the slightest use to appeal to the Bellman about it—he would only refer to his Naval Code, and read out in pathetic tones Admiralty Instructions which none of them had ever been able to understand—so it generally ended in its being fastened on, anyhow, across the rudder. The helmsman used to stand by with tears in his eyes; *he* knew it was all wrong, but alas! Rule 42 of the Code, 'No one shall speak to the Man at the Helm', had been completed by the Bellman himself with the words 'and the Man at the Helm shall speak to no one'. So remonstrance was impossible, and no steering could be done till the next varnishing day. During these bewildering intervals the ship usually sailed backwards.

As this poem is to some extent connected with the lay of the Jabberwock, let me take this opportunity of answering a question that has often been asked me, how to pronounce 'slithy toves'. The 'i' in 'slithy' is long, as in 'writhe'; and 'toves' is pronounced so as to rhyme with 'groves'. Again, the first 'o' in 'borogoves' is pronounced like the 'o' in 'borrow'. I have heard people try to

give it the sound of the 'o' in 'worry'. Such is Human Perversity.

This also seems a fitting occasion to notice the other hard words in that poem. Humpty-Dumpty's theory, of two meanings packed into one word like a portmanteau, seems to me the right explanation for all.

For instance, take the two words 'fuming' and 'furious'. Make up your mind that you will say both words, but leave it unsettled which you will say first. Now open your mouth and speak. If your thoughts incline ever so little towards 'fuming', you will say 'fuming-furious'; if they turn, by even a hair's breadth, towards 'furious', you will say 'furious-fuming'; but if you have the rarest of gifts, a perfectly balanced mind, you will say 'frumious'.

Supposing that, when Pistol uttered the well-known words 'Under which king, Bezonian? Speak or die!', Justice Shallow had felt certain that it was either William or Richard, but had not been able to settle which, so that he could not possibly say either name before the other, can it be doubted that, rather than die, he would have gasped out 'Rilchiam'!

Lewis Carroll

The Railway Juggernaut

Victims of the railway boom

The enigma that is the Boots

Nothing has created more controversy than the identity of this young man. After extensive research I have as yet been unable to find any verifiable evidence of his existence in official or civic documents from the period, although there are some intriguing leads that may yet bear fruit.

There has been the usual rash of unsubstantiated claims and conspiracy theories that one finds with historical figures of note. One woman insists the Boots was her Great-great-uncle Spenser, and her claim for custody of the diary and associated royalties is still before the courts.

That he was a young man at the inception of the expedition, probably in his early twenties, is apparent from the glimpse he provides of himself in his sketches. He is of slight build, tall, with a shock of dark, somewhat unruly hair. He refers to himself in the crew list as a 'Boots', a lowly occupation involving shining shoes or working as a general dogsbody in a hotel. However,

his facility with language, a pencil and paints would indicate a reasonable education.

Just why an educated young man should have been reduced to earning his living as a 'boots' on the streets of Oxford is a mystery. There have been many theories over the years but the most convincing is that he came from a well-to-do family that fell upon hard times. One of the powerful themes in this adventure is the advent of the steam engine, which, although providing many benefits (witness the train journey from Oxford to Bristol and the hybrid sail/steam vessel employed for the voyage) also led to the ruination of many middle-class families who had invested in the volatile railway boom of the period. Many fledgling companies went bankrupt, sending their shareholders to the poorhouse. It is possible Carroll's phrase 'to threaten its life with a railway-share' had a very personal and bitter meaning for the young man.

Given that scenario, and were he forced to eke out a living cleaning shoes and perhaps selling the odd drawing in the street, one can easily understand how

the Boots might jump at the chance to become part of any expedition, no matter how misguided.

This was, after all, an era of great discoveries. Fame, fortune and lecture tours awaited explorers returning from the far ends of the Earth with exotic botanical and zoological specimens. A young artist's reputation could be made almost overnight if he were diligent—and in the right place at the right time. There is evidence of a growing ambition in this respect, for the Boots' drawings, which at the start constitute straightforward objective recording of events and flora and fauna, come to include more and more images of himself in the latter pages of his journal.

However, I cannot go along with the cynical theory that a desire to portray himself as an intrepid explorer was behind the Boots' decision to continue the search for the missing Baker. This, I maintain, was a brave and altruistic act. His courage is again proven by his actions over those last dreadful days of the return voyage and his willingness to make the ultimate sacrifice for his beloved homeland.

LEWIS CARROLL IN 1855, AGED 23

LEWIS CARROLL

Lewis Carroll's real name was Charles Lutwidge Dodgson, and many, many books have examined his past in microscopic detail. But not one of them mentions the Boots' journal. Is this a well-orchestrated conspiracy? I don't believe so. I think that most—if not all—of his biographers and other historians were genuinely ignorant of its existence.

As we have seen from the furore that has ensued since this book was first published, however, there are those who have a vested interest in suppressing the revelations it contains. They have done their best to discredit the facts presented.

The intriguing question is whether the young Dodgson/Carroll himself ever came into contact with the Boots. I believe a meeting must have taken place, between Carroll and either the young artist/adventurer or someone who knew him and his story. There are just too many allusions and hints in the Carroll texts for us not to suspect a deeper knowledge behind his writing.

THE BOOTS' JOURNAL

I have already suggested that Dodgson, as a young student at Oxford, may have had his own misgivings about the Boots' account. The Boots was, after all, the sole survivor of the expedition and there is little if any evidence of the truth of his story other than his journal. British chapbooks of the period were full of bogus stories of exploration and adventure, and even if Carroll were himself convinced, he would still have faced the scepticism of his peers and mentors. It is probable that he did not want to jeopardise a promising future by publicly associating himself with a story of dubious origins. Far better to hide the journal away and provide himself with years of fun cloaking the historical facts in nonsense rhyme.

THE JOURNAL'S PROVENANCE

Since (either by accident or design) there is no mention of the journal in Charles Dodgson's effects or his will, some believe we may have more success in tracing its provenance from the final known link—the detestable Clutch. Just how the journal came into the hands of this man, however, also remains a mystery.

Clutch was a thief, a fact well known in collecting circles. He thought nothing of purloining anything he coveted and could not buy for a pittance, and I'm ashamed to admit it was the marvellous quality of the collection he had amassed by these dubious means that first attracted my attention.

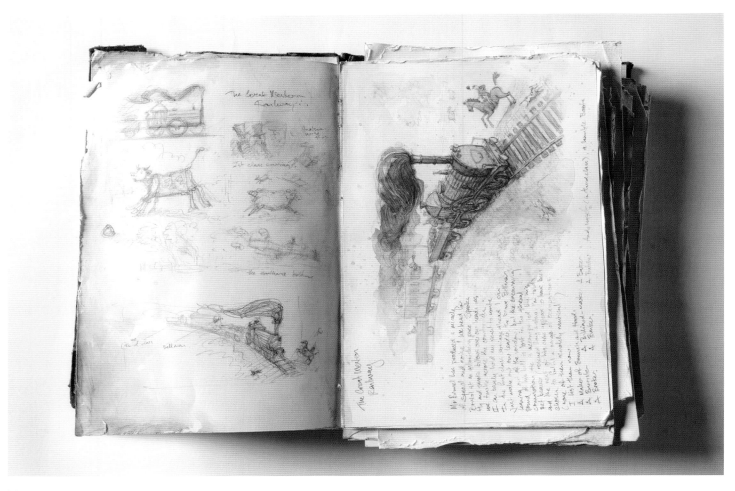

THE BOOTS' JOURNAL

Although I have been unsuccessful so far, perhaps a careful scrutiny of documented thefts from auction houses, libraries, museums and private collections might lead us first to the hatbox, since that is quite obviously a genuine 19th-century collectible (likely the property of the deceased Bellman). From there we could attempt to establish a link to Dodgson. This would go a long way to silencing the critics and naysayers.

THE ILLUSTRATIONS

My philosophy throughout this book has always been to present the Boots' story as clearly as possible so the reader may reach his or her own conclusions as to its veracity. This has meant transcribing his sometimes almost illegible script, and selecting the better images to illustrate the story. Some sceptics, however, have used the dearth of raw images from the journal to cast doubt on its being a genuine artefact. In response I include, in this 42nd edition, several of the Boots' rough drawings and present these photographs of selected page spreads taken from the journal in their original form.

Once one is able to get past the dilapidated condition of the journal the Boots' intention becomes clear. From his sketches, notes and composition studies it seems obvious that right from the start of the expedition he planned to publish a lavishly illustrated account on his return. Examples of more finished art were found on larger sheets of paper no doubt taken along for the purpose. I suspect that in those last dreadful days the artist cut, folded and inserted these more polished efforts into his working journal for safekeeping.

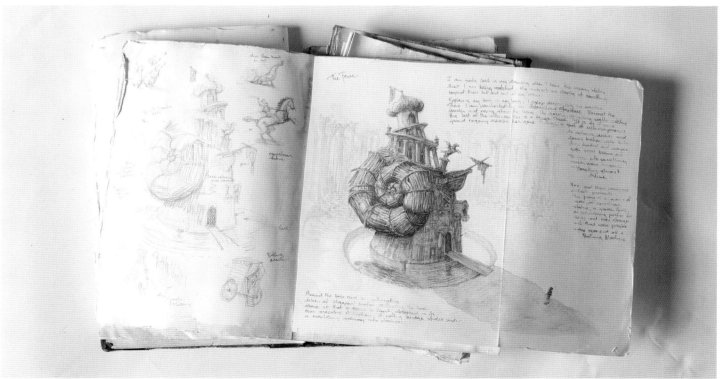

DR WILLIAM BUCKLAND

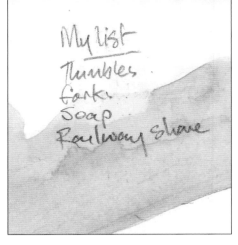

THE BOOTS' LIST

OBAYSCH DANCES THE HIPPOPOTAMUS POLKA

THE LECTURE

'The stomach rules the world' is a phrase most commonly associated with the Very Reverend Dr William Buckland (1784–1856), a prominent Oxford clergyman, scientist and enthusiastic zoophagist (eater of wild animals). I am reliably informed that London Zoo often sent its deceased inmates up to the good doctor in case he wished to taste them.

Dr Buckland, Canon of Christ Church and later Dean of Westminster, famously excavated what he claimed were antediluvian hyena bones in Kirkdale Cave in Yorkshire in 1822. He also had a pet hyena called Billy. The influence of William and his son Frank (who owned a pet bear called Tiglath-Pileser) on Carroll's version of this tragic tale should not be underestimated. Carroll, who also lived in Oxford, would have been aware of Dr Buckland's discoveries and theories in natural history. It is also interesting to note that in his official portrait, Buckland holds a shell.

It is apparent from the Boots' sketch, however, that it is not Buckland who is holding forth at this particular lecture with the magic lantern, but someone wearing a bicorne hat and dangling what appears to be a bell from his hand … the celebrated Bellman, that peculiar mix of determination and incompetence, who was to lead the expedition.

N.B. There is no known record of an aardvark (as depicted in the lantern slide), for steaming or any other purpose, being sent to Oxford from London Zoo.

THE BOOTS' LIST

At the end of the story we find that two of the things on this strange list of equipment—the railway-shares and the thimbles—were ultimately of great assistance to the Boots in his identification of the Snark at the end of the voyage. I presume the instructions to take these objects came from the Bellman. If so, they were a flash of inspiration in an otherwise confused and ill-considered enterprise.

TIMING AND HISTORICAL CONTEXT

There have been numerous attempts to pinpoint a date for the expedition and this continues to be a field ripe for further investigation. What we do know is that it must have taken place—and the Boots' journal must have made its way into the hands of the young Oxford graduate Lewis Carroll—sometime before 1855, when the first stanza of *Jabberwocky* appeared in *Mischmasch*, a periodical Carroll wrote and illustrated for his family.

Just why he waited 16 years to publish the completed poem in *Through the Looking-Glass and What Alice Found There*, and then a further five years before revealing his version of the entire expedition in *The Hunting of the Snark* in 1876, is another matter for conjecture.

To put the venture into some sort of historical context we should remember that this period coincides with Livingstone's exploration of central Africa, Wallace's collection of specimens up the Amazon River, and the arrival of Obaysch, the first hippopotamus at London Zoo.

THE *ACTAEON*

THE *COMET*

First Class politeness

Second Class politeness

Third Class politeness

THE RAILWAY CLASS SYSTEM

THE GREAT WESTERN RAILWAY

There are a number of inaccuracies and anomalies in this drawing. The Boots has drawn himself alone in an open third-class carriage; one would have thought perhaps the Billiard-marker and surely the Beaver (being, as it were, livestock) should have accompanied him.

Further, this is the very type of carriage the Railway Regulation Act of 1844 sought to eliminate. I suspect this drawing is therefore a deliberate falsehood in an attempt at sardonic humour by our young artist. (If not, I hope the incident was reported to the authorities at the time.)

The detail (as shown on page 17) of the startled huntsman with his dogs is typical of the deprecating way the new railways of the period were portrayed.

Although one hesitates to identify the train from such a fleeting impression, it is possible that the Boots has drawn the *Actaeon*, one of the Firefly class of locomotives built for the Great Western

Railway by Daniel Gooch between 1840 and 1842. If so there is a deep irony here, for the legendary hero Actaeon was transformed into a stag and torn to pieces by his own hounds. Thus, in a strange parallel to our crew's fate in their quest for the Snark, the hunter became the hunted.

THE SHIP

The ship appears to be a small steam- and wind-powered vessel designed along the lines of the early merchant steamship *Comet* (Glasgow, 1812), although presumably with a much deeper draught to accommodate the crew's quarters and stores. The innovation of the 'Great Couch' on the poop deck comes as a surprise; it would seem more at home in a gentlemen's club than on a vessel undertaking a serious voyage.

With its limited fuel range, the crew would have had to rely heavily on sailpower on a long voyage, using the ship's engines only when necessary.

THE SNARK-COOKER

THE SNARK-COOKER

The large, apparently mechanical object the crew is struggling with is clearly intended as a Snark cooking device, although its effectiveness is somewhat suspect. Although the Bellman asserts that it will be essential for 'steeping' their prize, how he has come to this notion as the correct method of preparing a Snark for consumption is not clear. The cooker appears to have been constructed in almost total ignorance of the size, shape and nature of the quarry, presumably in an attempt to cover all eventualities (and make a nice cup of tea whilst one waits). It was designed, one suspects, by the Bellman, and appears to work on steam pressure controlled by a series of pulleys, wheels and, of course, bells.

THE EMBARKATION POINT

From a study of the railway routes of the period and the outline of what appears to be Flat Holm island with its lighthouse on the southwestern tip in

DIAGRAM OF THE TIDE AT CLEVELAND BEACH AND THE SHIP

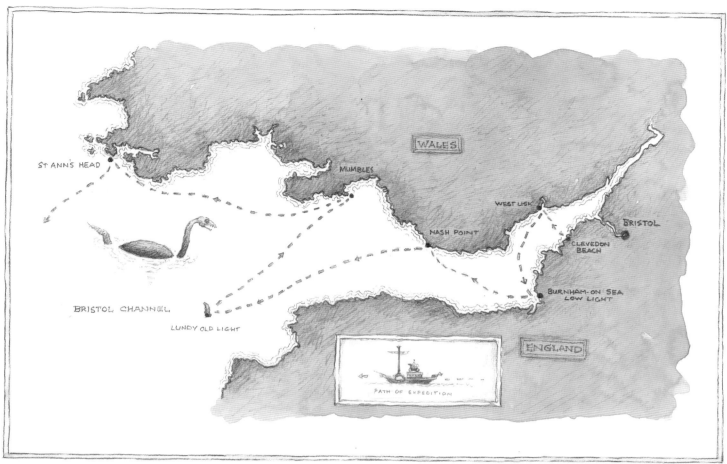

THE EXPEDITION'S COURSE ACROSS THE BRISTOL CHANNEL, AND (BELOW) THE LIGHTHOUSES

the background of the Boots' drawing on page 41, the beach can probably be identified as Clevedon, on the coast of the Severn Estuary, south of Bristol. The tidal range in the estuary is one of the highest in the world, up to 15 metres, and it would have totally submerged the poorly loaded Bellman's ship at its peak.

THE LIGHTHOUSES

It is difficult to know for certain who is to blame for the meandering and dangerous course followed in the early part of the expedition. Whether as a result of the inexperience of the young Boots as helmsman or the inexplicable commands of his captain, their ship seems to have arrived unerringly at several rocky sections of the coastline so treacherous that they warranted lighthouses.

That the Bellman should then insist they linger in their predicament, endeavouring to look their best, beggars belief, but the evidence in the Boots' journal is clear. Our young artist obviously had time to sketch several of these warning lights and, in doing so, has left us with a record of the expedition's haphazard progress across the Bristol Channel.

Taken in the order they appear in his journal the lights are: West Usk, Burnham-on-Sea Low Light, Nash Point, Lundy, Mumbles, St Ann's Head.

Benjamin Waterhouse Hawkins' ichthyosaur

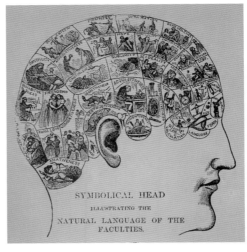

Dr Gall's Symbolical Head

Pig overboard

The sketch on pages 22–23 depicting the rash escape and imagined fate of the expedition's pig is uncharacteristically whimsical and possibly points to a familiarity with Thomas Hawkins' hugely popular work *The Book of Great Sea Dragons* (1840), in particular the frontispiece by John Martin.

More intriguingly, however, as several correspondents have pointed out, the huge pig-devouring monster also strangely anticipates the ichthyosaur sculpted by Hawkins' son, Benjamin Waterhouse Hawkins, that was unveiled to the public in Crystal Palace Park in 1854. Was there time for the Boots to see this work before he joined the expedition? There had been many important plesiosaur and ichthyosaur fossil finds along the western coastline of the Bristol Channel, and indeed the Boots may have seen examples in the collection at Bristol Institution as he passed through the city. Is this simply a case of the young artist and the established sculptor both responding to the recent paleontological finds or is there a deeper connection? Had the Boots had privileged access to Waterhouse Hawkins'

studio or perhaps early sketches?

There is another interesting aspect to consider. There was a belief in some quarters at the time that these prehistoric creatures, the bones of which were sensationally emerging from the earth all over Britain, might still in fact exist. Given that the Bristol Channel coast, in fact Bristol itself, was famous for these artefacts, it is possible the sea monster sketch masks an underlying anxiety on the part of the artist—a premonition of the zoological terrors to come?

Dr Gall's phrenology

Dr Franz Joseph Gall is considered the father of phrenology, a pseudo-scientific 19th-century belief that measurement of the skull could determine an individual's psychological attributes. The young Boots' views of the compartmentalised ship does indeed resemble the then-popular charts and models of heads divided into sectors dedicated to particular vices or virtues.

The Boots has no doubt gleaned some amusement from allotting his fellow crew members their qualities and failings as labelled on his chart. It is interesting

to speculate, as some have, that this is where Carroll may have got many of the character descriptions that appear in the early stanzas of *The Hunting of the Snark*. It is certainly worthwhile considering the young artist-cum-helmsman's labelling of himself as 'Frustration' when reading Carroll's Preface: 'The Helmsman used to stand by with tears in his eyes; *he* knew it was all wrong, but alas!'

The Beaver

There are two extant species of beaver: *Castor fiber* (the Eurasian beaver) and *Castor canadensis* (North American beaver). It would appear from the Bellman's comments on page 29 that his is the latter variety. As an economist from Halifax has pointed out, it is worthwhile noting the huge contribution this animal was making (one would think reluctantly) to the economy of Canada at the time through the provision of pelts used in the manufacture of hats.

Just how this particular beaver came into the Bellman's keeping is an intriguing matter. The Boots mentions he had heard that it 'was rescued from a stew', and

THE BAKER IN A GALE

SMALL SHELLS AT THE SHORELINE

BEAVER HATS OF THE PERIOD, FROM TOP: THE WELLINGTON (1812), THE PARIS BEAU (1815), THE D'ORSAY (1820), THE REGENT (1825)

Carroll adds that it was 'a tame one he [the Bellman] had of his own/ Whose death would be deeply deplored'. The Bellman certainly seems fond of the animal and one wonders if the Beaver's later befriending of the Butcher did not lead to some jealousy.

THE BAKER

One particular expert on Victorian men's fashion has raised the possibility that rather than feeling the cold, as the Boots supposes, the Baker wore many coats so he was well prepared for every social eventuality. Gentlemen's etiquette of the period required different coats for different occasions and times of the day. I offer this snippet from *The Habits of Good Society* (1859): 'There are four kinds of coats which a well-dressed man must have: a morning coat, a frock coat, a dress coat, and an overcoat.' To that we might add a waistcoat and the traditional white double-breasted baker's coat.

It could be that the Baker, to avoid continually having to return to his cabin to change, chose to wear them all simultaneously.

In the Boots' drawing of the Baker at the deck rail his overcoat is revealed as cut in the 'Noah's Ark' style (appropriately, given the later turn of events), and the ensemble is completed by a Spanish circular cloak.

His outer boots are Wellingtons, befitting such a truly British enterprise.

THE LANDING

The Boots appears to have recorded very little of the hunt itself in his notes. Perhaps, caught up in the heat of the moment(s), he opted instead for quick sketches of the incidents he witnessed.

There is one short, disparaging description of the landing beach, which hints at the demeanour of the crew and, perhaps most significantly, provides a first mention of the curious shells:

We have waded ashore into a most unfortunate situation. A sharp wind cuts down the channel, driving blasts of sand across a beach surrounded by forbidding cliffs. To one side is a stagnant, insect-infested creek that seeps from a dark valley.

Our captain mustered us all on the sand for a roll call, ringing his bell encouragingly, but I am sorry to report there were some dark mutterings among the crew.

I myself kept up my spirits by investigating our new surroundings and was soon rewarded by the discovery of several small, strangely decorated shells at the shoreline.

195

Pirate with pigtails

The Baker's boxes

The Broker's hair

The twisted tower of hair the Boots depicts on the head of the Broker continues to mystify. Carroll, of course, conjures up his fantastical scenario: that this is the result of the Bellman's novel method of landing the crew, 'supporting each man on the top of the tide by a finger entwined in his hair'. However, if that were the case, why do the rest of the explorers not sport similar hairdos, and why should the Broker's spiralling locks alone persist throughout the expedition? The Boots noted a 'sharp wind' on the beach when they went ashore, but this should surely have affected everyone's coiffure equally.

The only explanation that comes close to being acceptable has been suggested by a marine historian from the Bahamas. He is reminded of an old buccaneer's remedy for lice, which involved combing tar into the seaman's infested hair. Apparently the stiffened, rope-like result was often twisted into a decorative pigtail. It is possible, just possible, that this is what the Broker had in mind, but I have problems reconciling the image of a pigtailed buccaneer with the pallid and ineffectual Broker who appears in the Boots' drawings.

The Baker's boxes

He could only bake Bride-cake—for which, I may state,
No materials were to be had.

Is Carroll suggesting the boxes of supplies, so helpfully removed from Cleveland Beach by a local fisherman, contained baking supplies? (We know at least one box contained soap—see page 198.)

Hyenas and bears

He would joke with hyænas, returning their stare
And he once went a walk, paw-in-paw, with a bear …

We have already noted the influence of William and Frank Buckland and their adventures with those creatures on this story (see The Lecture, page 188).

Conybeare's cave at Kirkdale

A FISH-SKIN HELMET FROM THE PACIFIC

THE DAGGER-PROOF COAT

The Beaver's best course was, no doubt, to procure
A second-hand dagger-proof coat—
So the Baker advised it—and next, to insure
Its life in some Office of note:

There is certainly the possibility—you might say expectation—that expedition members would have equipped themselves with some sort of protective clothing. Given the unknown nature of the threat they faced, we can only imagine the wonderful variety of forms that clothing might have taken. Disappointingly, however, there is no evidence of such in the Boots' journal, and certainly no depiction of a dagger-proof coat, second-hand or otherwise.

Insurance, though, is another matter, and a policy may well have been available from either the Banker or the Broker. Presumably the Bellman, as the owner of the Beaver, would have been the principal beneficiary, but sadly, as we now know, he was unable to collect on any claim he might have made.

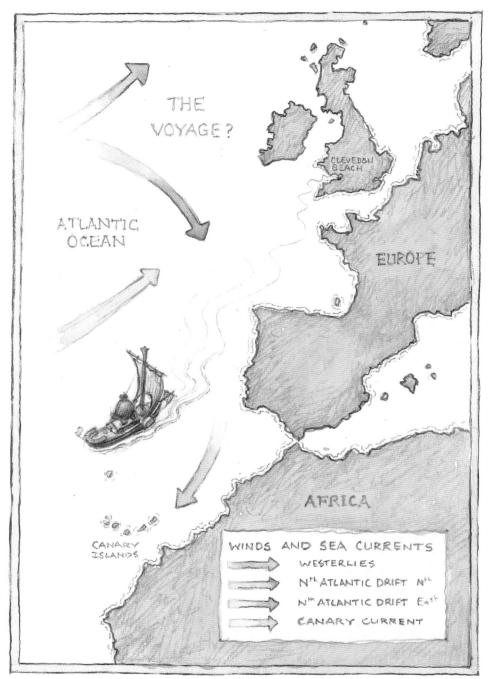

WINDS AND CURRENTS IN THE NORTHEAST ATLANTIC

THE MAP

The 'blank' map Carroll would have us believe the Bellman used is of course purely his way of saying he has no idea where the expedition went. From the vague information we have, we can only guess at the course of the voyage and the whereabouts of the island.

As noted earlier, the expedition left Clevedon and spent some time

THE EXPEDITION VESSEL CARRIED AGAINST THE WIND—IN CARROLL'S WORDS, 'SNARKED'

zigzagging between lighthouses across the Bristol Channel. Given this haphazard mode of navigation, any real progress was more likely due to the effect of winds, tides and currents than any actual purposeful sailing.

Taking that into account it would be reasonable to propose that the vessel became caught up in the southeast branch of the North Atlantic Drift, then ventured on to the Canary Current coursing south along the coast of northwest Africa. There are certainly reports of lost and fabulous islands in this area, many with chasms and crags. There are also notorious areas where the current may be stronger than the wind, where a vessel may find itself in the alarming situation of sailing backwards. This is no doubt Carroll's inspiration for the Bellman's statement:

*Said he **had** hoped, at least, when the wind blew due East,*
*That the ship would **not** travel due West!*

The possibility that the expedition did in fact drift far further than these islands is discussed on page 201.

THE SAILING

The principal failing occurred in the sailing
…

It is difficult to imagine a more incompetent captain or indeed crew. The Boots has already drawn our attention to the dependence of the Bellman on the Naval Code for handling the craft. Add to that his constant arbitrary bell-ringing, which must have terribly confused the various 'watches' on board, and the inexperience of his helmsman (the Boots), and we have a recipe for disaster.

A SNARK TRAP

FAINTING FOR EFFECT

TRAPS AND CAGES

A number of traps and cages feature in the background of the Boots' sketch of the Bellman's speech. This is in keeping with the Boots' statement that part of the expedition's goal was to take live specimens back to England for possible acclimatisation and eventually to 'enrich the plates of England'.

The variety of shapes, sizes and types is consistent with our observations regarding the Snark-cooker, indicating the same general ignorance of the prey. Among other apparatus we can see a box with a stick and string, a lobster pot, a spade for digging holes, a tethered chicken, a lasso and, more significantly, a miniature bathing-machine. This last, one suspects, is another of the Bellman's contraptions (note the bell that signals the Snark's capture).

BATHING-MACHINES

Bathing-machines, as I'm sure you know, were 'disrobing carriages' to facilitate discreet bathing, and were very much part of the British fashionable seaside resort scene throughout the 19th century.

The Snark's fondness for them, as mentioned by Carroll, may not have arisen from its belief that they add to the 'beauty of scenes', but for another reason entirely, a much more delicate function that I will discuss later.

A BATHING-MACHINE

FAINTING AWAY

I am indebted to a correspondent from Cambridge who has pointed out that the Baker may have been suffering from an affliction more usually associated at the time with women. 'Swooning' was common among fashionable women and girls, due to the 'burden' of their underclothing, particularly their tight corsets. In *The Girl's Book of Diversions* (1835) by Eliza Leslie and Lydia Marie Child, we even find instruction on how to faint for effect. The correspondent suggests the Baker's swoon may simply have been the natural consequence of too many tight coats, or perhaps a tad too much grog.

Frontispiece to Hawkins' book

Kilsby Tunnel, 1852

Antediluvian

'Antediluvian' refers to that period in the Bible between the creation of the Earth and the great flood. An 'antediluvian tone' is more difficult to define; however, I suspect something like this passage, from our friend Thomas Hawkins' *The Book of the Great Sea-Dragons* (1840), if read out in a low and mournful way, might fit the bill:

But the Awful Wrecks compassing us round about, and restless Eld murmuring ever in our ear, and abhorrent Heaven himself, eclipsed, but not extinguished, protest against the cheerless Spirit of Knowledge, by which all Things are referred to insensate Matter and icy Dream; and beckon us from the Paradise of Fools, within whose Magic Circle so many Souls have madly staked and lost their all …

Pears' Soap advertisement

Soap

There is at least one box clearly marked 'soap' in the Boots' sketch of the Baker awaiting embarkation on Clevedon Beach. Soap was often seen as a symbol for progress and the 'civilising mission' of Empire and trade, and it would have been quite in order for the Snark expedition to carry quantities of the stuff into unexplored territory. Carroll alludes to this practice when he writes, 'you may charm it with smiles and soap.'

Its effectiveness against wild animals is open to debate, but it may have been thought to be of interest to a Snark and therefore attractive as bait (for example in the bathing-machine trap).

Railway-shares

You may threaten its life with a railway-share …

As previously mentioned, it is possible the Boots' family was one of many who lost their fortunes through the collapse of the railway boom, leading to his drastically reduced circumstances. It is perhaps ironic, then, that his last drawings were sketched on the back of share certificates abandoned on the deck of the doomed ship.

The reason for the Snarks' fear of these pieces of paper remains as much a mystery today as it was to the young artist. Perhaps it was the risk associated with the construction of the railways themselves. The tunnels in this era were particularly hazardous, being prone to collapse, seeping sewage, gas, water and quicksand. For a creature such as the Snark, fond as it clearly was of hollow spaces, any of these might have been a terrifying prospect.

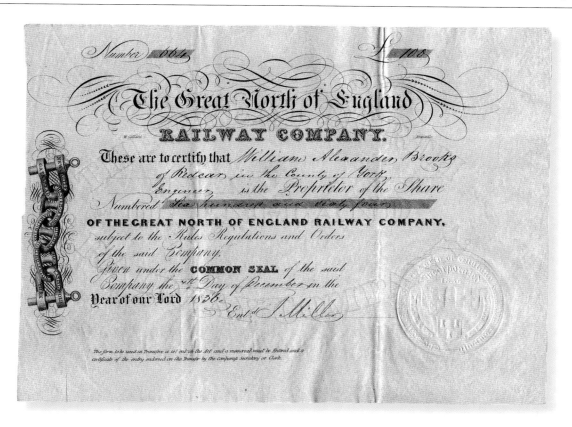

ANTIQUE RAILWAY-SHARE CERTIFICATE, FRONT AND BACK (AS DECORATED BY THE BOOTS)

THE BIRD CHART – LEFT TO RIGHT: THE GREAT AUK, THE DODO, THE ELEPHANT BIRD, THE MOA, THE JUBJUB BIRD

THE BIRD CHART

This chart shows an estimate of size of the Jubjub bird relative to other birds that have had the misfortune to come under the culinary scrutiny of mankind (and are consequently now extinct). As the reader can see, the Jubjub is altogether a much grander creature and it is to be hoped it has not suffered the same fate. Perhaps if the Snark expedition had fulfilled its goals this fashionable bird would have been next on the menu.

THIMBLES

The thimbles the Boots dutifully carried would eventually prove invaluable to him in identifying the Snarks. Given the creatures' enthusiasm for them, we can probably deduce they were of the shell-like closed dressmaker's type rather than the open-ended tailor's variety. The likelihood that the thimbles were made of silver and therefore shiny would have added to their allure.

ANTIQUE THIMBLE

TRANSPORTATION

'Transportation for life' was the sentence it gave …

It is tempting to think that Carroll was alluding to the escape of the expedition's pig when he charged his fictitious porker with deserting its sty in 'The Barrister's Dream'. That poor animal is eventually sentenced to 'transportation for life', a punishment that would have had the same sad outcome for either creature. Carroll's pig handily pre-empted that fate of course by already being dead.

'Transportation for life' was a common sentence for petty crime during this period and would likely have involved a long and arduous voyage to the Swan River colony in western Australia. The chances of a tasty-looking pig surviving that journey on a ship full of hungry convicts would be slim at best. It might, however, have got in a couple of verses of 'Botany Bay' before the knife fell:

Farewell to old England forever,
Farewell to my rum culls as well.
Farewell to the well-known Old Bailey
Where I used for to cut such a swell.

The fog-bound three-masted merchantman sketched by the Boots may

THREE-MASTED MERCHANTMAN IN FOG

THE THYLACINE

well have been a convict ship sighted by our adventurers en route. The ships used for transportation were often privately owned merchant vessels chartered by the British government. We can only speculate on the fate of the expedition's pig after its first transgression. It could well have been arrested, tried at sea and kept in chains on board that very vessel.

As a reader from Adelaide has pointed out, if this was indeed a passing convict ship, the Boots' drawing certainly lends weight to the argument that his craft was pursuing a well-established route to the Antipodes.

THE BANDERSNATCH

Correspondence I have received has pointed out that here we have evidence of a striped dog-like creature that could be mistaken for a hyena.

For my part, however, I think this sketch leans more towards a thylacine, or Tasmanian tiger. A thylacine was exhibited at London Zoo in 1850: perhaps the Boots visited personally or saw it in souvenir reproductions or prints.

His brief glimpse of the creature that attacked the Banker may have convinced the Boots he had seen the same animal before. We can see from this photograph that the creature certainly had very distinctive and fearsome gaping jaws. Carroll, in his Preface to *The Hunting of the Snark*, describes the Bandersnatch's yawning mouthful of sharp teeth as 'frumious'. Quite so.

A LONGER VOYAGE?

The possibility that the Bandersnatch is in fact a thylacine brings us to the argument for a far longer voyage than originally thought: all the way to the Antipodes. The Jubjub bird in a certain light might resemble the emu of Australia or even the great moa of New Zealand (see previous page).

Could the expedition have meandered this far? It would require the ship to have wandered through equatorial waters into the Brazil Current, which could have carried it to the Cape of Good Hope where it could have fallen prey to the Antarctic Circumpolar Current. As

unlikely as this sounds, this is the very route (dubbed the Great Circle) that the supposed convict ship would have taken to the Antipodes.

Detractors have pointed out that there is no mention of the winds, icebergs and wild seas the crew would have encountered on such a voyage through the Roaring Forties. To counter that argument, some point to Carroll's lines from the Bellman's speech: 'We have sailed many months …' A typical voyage between Britain and Australia in the 1850s took two to four months (a period we would have to extend significantly due to the ineptitude of the crew).

There is further argument here for a longer voyage into the southern seas. Since the crew had no set course on their outward voyage, and indeed seemed to be carried by currents and winds to the island, it is difficult to imagine them returning to their home port against the same prevailing conditions. It is far more likely they followed the Great Circle route around Cape Horn and back to England.

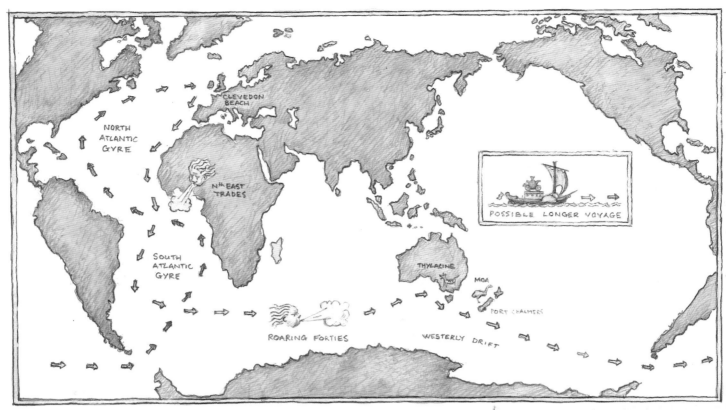

THE GREAT CIRCLE ROUTE

THE ISLAND

The Boots drew a more comprehensive map of the island from his sketches and I include it here so readers may come to their own conclusions as to the landform's geological (or, as the Boots suggests, biological) origins. It certainly does have a perplexing appearance. First impressions might lead one to suspect it is volcanic in origin, and the cove occupied by the expedition vessel a caldera breached by the sea. However, there is no denying there is something disturbingly organic about its underlying spiral formation; this intriguing aspect might be investigated by a future expedition.

The island

THE TULGEY WOOD

Lewis Carroll aptly named the densely forested area in the centre of the island 'the tulgey wood'. The poet managed to evoke some of the trepidation the Boots must have felt on entering this dank and odoriferous jungle.

It must be one of science's greatest disappointments that none of the Boots' collection of plant samples and seeds survived. The few sketches we have are tantalisingly vague, although they seem to depict new (and in the case of the plant one suspects inspired Carroll's Tumtum tree, frankly unbelievable) species. The botanists I have consulted so far—perhaps afraid of controversy or, worse still, ridicule—are reluctant to commit themselves to any sort of classification, and so, sadly, the matter must rest unless further evidence (or a courageous authority) comes to light.

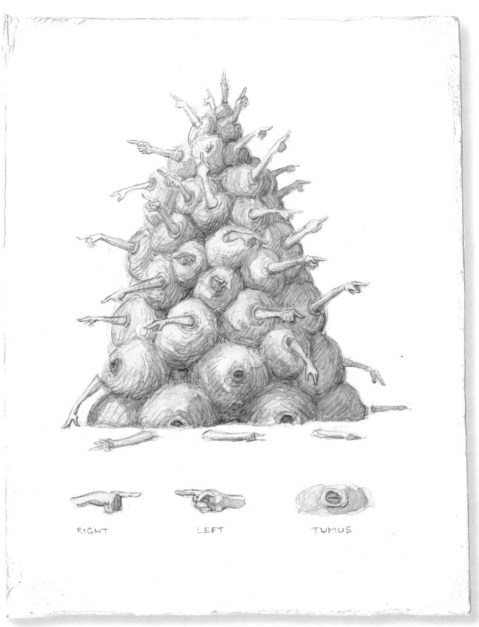

RIGHT   LEFT   TUMUS

Tumtum tree

TOVES?

BOROGOVES?

THE WABE: TOVES, BOROGOVES AND RATHS

In the ruined garden our budding natural history illustrator really came to the fore. The Boots must have sensed a unique opportunity here to collect information on hitherto undiscovered species to present to the scientific community on his return to England. He not only recorded their appearance but also made notes on their demeanour and behaviour, and it seems fairly obvious that Carroll used these drawings and observations when naming and describing the animals in his whimsical private periodical *Mischmasch* in 1855. His statements on the diet of these animals are, of course, pure conjecture:

Tove: A species of white badger. They had smooth white hair, long hind legs and short horns like a stag: lived chiefly on cheese. (Carroll mistakes what are plainly tufts of fur on the animal's head for horns.)

Borogove: An extinct kind of parrot. They had no wings, beaks turned up, and made their nest under sundials: lived on veal. (They were clearly not extinct or possessed of an upturned beak. Careful scrutiny reveals tiny vestigial wings.)

RATHS?

VICTORIAN SUNDIAL

Rath: *A species of land turtle. Head erect, mouth like a shark: forelegs curved out so that the animal walked on its knees, smooth green body: lived on swallows and oysters.* (This last description is plainly wrong and Carroll takes the opportunity in Alice's conversation with Humpty Dumpty in *Through the Looking-Glass and What Alice Found There* to correct himself: 'Well, a rath is a kind of green pig …' states Humpty Dumpty.)

The Boots also records the badger-like creatures as leaping about, the parrots as ragged and the pigs as distraught and wailing. These behaviours Carroll describes in *Jabberwocky* as 'gyring and gimbling', 'mimsy', 'outgrabing' respectively.

Pursuing the theory that the island is somewhere in Australasia, the identification of these species has been problematic. On consulting Menkhorst and Knight's *A Field Guide to the Mammals of Australia* (2010), I find several animals with badger-like stripes, and many with long hind legs, but, disappointingly, none with both—and certainly none with horns or horn-like tufts as well.

With regard to the raths, Carroll's description is whimsical as these pigs are clearly not green (unless there has been substantial fading of the pigment over time). This could lead us to conclude that they are a common variety of pig imported to the island by the builders of the pavilion and intended for the table. However, their elongated snouts are curious. One correspondent wonders if this could be the result of prolonged snivelling.

Borogoves are an easier proposition. A quick thumb through Simpson and Day's *A Field Guide to the Birds of Australia* (2010) reveals any number of candidates. In New Zealand, if we exclude the kea and the kākā, which never look in the least 'mimsy', we are left with the kākāpo, which sometimes does, and has only recently been saved from extinction.

THE SUNDIALS

Needless to say, it is very unusual to have so many sundials assembled in one place, and several of my collector friends have suggested that this might be evidence of the presence of an early horologist or timepiece collector. A psychiatrist from Minsk is convinced it is symptomatic of chronophobia, the frantic need to keep checking and cross-checking the time. Possibly the afflicted person would also be loaded down with pocket-watches and have a houseful of grandfather clocks.

Whoever was responsible had clearly departed by the time the Boots arrived because the collection had fallen into disrepair, with sundials teetering at odd angles and creatures nesting freely beneath them.

It is almost certainly this slovenly attitude to time that inspired Carroll to observe of the Snark:

Its habit of getting up late you'll agree,
It carries too far, when I say,
That it frequently breakfasts at five o'clock tea
And dines on the following day.

A SELECTION OF SHELLS

THE TOWER

I think we must accept the Boots' assertion that the tower was the work of a Boojum—in fact *the* Boojum, as the absence of the creature during the Boots' night of terror in the tower backs up the theory that it had already embarked on its mission to stow away on the ship.

The tower with its spiralling shell-like core and array of columns—not to mention the turret cannibalised from the pavilion—the Boots believes is the handiwork of a grotesquely enlarged Snark. Here, though, its 'shell' is so huge the animal could not possibly carry it on its back, and the pillaged architectural accretions seem selected as trappings of power rather than mere ornament. The ship's prow is a mystery, but both the fork and the soap advertisement remind us of the Boots' list, and the bathing-machine is perhaps to be expected. The equestrian statue we now know has much more sinister implications.

From the Boots' description the interior walls have remained pure shell, covered in layers of pearly secretions with extraordinary qualities. To all intents and purposes the tower appears to be half building, half beast.

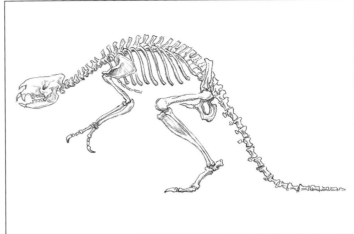

Sons of the Empire

PROCOPTODON JABBERWOCKI?

SONS OF EMPIRE

What are we to make of those strange images the Boots frantically copied as they appeared inside the tower walls? Some people have gone so far as to suggest this whole episode resulted from a dream or a figment of our adventurer's wild imagination brought on by fatigue and stress: that somehow the anxieties of his day have produced a dark fantasy in his mind. Others have suggested he may have sampled some woodland plant with hallucinogenic properties.

Still others stoutly defend the Boots' thinking that what he observed, stored in the translucent layers of the tower's inner shell, was some sort of optical remnant of its victims, the original inhabitants of the cannibalised pavilion. It is an established fact that molluscs (to which family the creature is at least partly related) will react to irritations by smothering them with iridescent secretions. This is, after all, how pearls are formed. The escapades of the soldier might have been so hard to stomach that the Boojum covered them in lustrous nacre, leaving them to reflect endlessly back and forth until the Boots' lantern brought them into focus. The soldier's hunt for an exotic beast ends in the despatch of the hunted and the triumph of the hunter, a story repeated time and time again throughout this era.

One theory points to the fact that the men reconnoitering from their pavilion balcony in their military uniforms are the epitome of colonisation: the imperial compulsion to civilise and tame the savage wilderness, supplanting it with tended paths, gardens and decorative sundials.

THE JABBERWOCK

Considering the beast, the Jabberwock itself, we are once again faced with an uncanny resemblance to a Australasian creature—one that has supposedly been extinct for 30,000 years. In the Boots' hasty yet bone-chilling sketch of the animal as it confronts the horseman hero, it appears to be some sort of giant kangaroo. Many letters have pointed to the prehistoric *Procoptodon goliah* as an obvious candidate.

Detractors dismiss this theory, drawing attention to the creature's dinosaur-like tiptoe stance, but recent research reveals that *P. goliah* did indeed walk, rather than hop like a modern kangaroo. Add to that the single large toe on each hind foot and the two large claws ('that catch') on the forelimbs, and the argument is compelling. The large tail dragging behind could help explain the terrifying 'whiffling' noise heard by the Boots in his headlong dash from the forest (and subsequently appropriated by Carroll).

Many authorities believe that *P. goliah* survived well into the period of human existence in Australia and may be the inspiration behind Aboriginal stories of a fearsome 'fighting kangaroo'. Could a small pocket of these creatures have terrorised the island—and do they linger still?

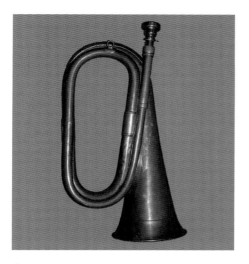

A MILITARY DOUBLE-COILED BUGLE

GASTROSHARKIS HERMITICUS SNARKI

THE BUGLE

I am grateful to an enthusiastic military historian from Bath who has, despite the transformation it has undergone, identified the bugle as an example of the copper single-coil type popular with British cavalry after 1812. The added twists and turns in its tubing, however, apparently surpass even those of the double-coiled bugle (1870) in complexity, and our historian is surprised it worked as well as it apparently did.

Along with offering a wealth of other information concerning battle sounds, horses, signals etc (in the way of military historians), he mentions the echoes created by the Boots' bugle blast among the chasms and crags. Apparently this duplicates the deception practised by one Canadian Colonel Charles de Salaberry on opposing American forces during the Battle of Chateauguay (1812). The good colonel, finding himself in the difficult position of trying to take an enemy forest with insufficient troops, deployed his buglers to sound the advance from a variety of hidden positions. The Americans, like our beast, assumed an attack on a broad front and were

fooled into retreat. It seems a tenuous connection but I promised I would mention it.

Just how this distorted and decorated instrument came to be in the tower is far more interesting. Its role in the development of a Boojum will be discussed later but it is interesting to note at this stage that while a bugle is clearly visible against the huntsman's saddle at the beginning of the hunt in the *Jabberwocky* drawings, it is absent on his triumphant return. One must assume the horn became detached in the mêlée, lost in the forest and left, as it were, for someone—or something—else to find.

GASTROSHARKIS HERMITICUS SNARKI

It is regrettable that the bugle has not survived for analysis. On the other hand, we must be grateful that even the drawing survived.

In his notes the Boots states that he drew *Gastrosharkis hermiticus snarki* as a duty to his fellow crewmates, to complete the hunt as it were. But surely his detailed depiction is more than that—it is a

clear attempt at correct natural history illustration.

Touchingly, it also gives us some indication of the limits of the young man's scientific knowledge. The Boots' attempt at biological labelling is admirable in intention; however, the species he has identified would place the island simultaneously on opposite sides of the Atlantic. Having said that, if the wing does belong to a swallow (albeit a very large one), that lends credence to his identification of the birds nesting on the cliffs near the ship's mooring.

The name itself is a little naïve. Academic opinion today tends towards *Gastroselachus crustpaguris*, but under the circumstances I think we can forgive the young man a few inaccuracies. After all, the drawing was completed under the most terrifying circumstances—as the last survivor on the ship and in the shadow of the Boojum.

It is a measure of the young man that he wanted to share the credit for discovering the Snark with his crewmates. For me, however, it is to the Boots and the Boots alone, for his courage and for his perseverance, that this honour should belong. Would that he had connected

211

QUEEN VICTORIA IN 1845, AGED 34

AN 1848 GROAT

his own name to this discovery, thereby revealing his identity so we could appropriately celebrate his achievements.

GREAT EXPECTATIONS

Many returning explorers of this period became celebrities overnight. They were in great demand for public talks and sometimes went on lecture tours the length and breadth of Britain. It was not uncommon for them even to gain a royal audience. The Boots is right, however, that the lack of even the slightest trace of a specimen would have been a distinct disadvantage. Given later developments, his comment is quite ironic.

SNAILS

The snails—or rather, as we now know, the Snarks—caused growing consternation as they increased in number and size on the return voyage. The time and attention the Boots devoted to recording the creatures and their activities betrays the growing unease

about their presence.

As it turned out, these studies were also an important step in the formulation of the Boots' later theories. It is interesting that on the island the decorations and adornments accrued by the creatures comprised mainly natural items (Carroll differentiated between 'those that have *feathers* and bite' and those 'that have *whiskers* and scratch'). On the ship, however, the snails show a marked interest—verging on covetousness—for man-made objects (thimbles, the Barrister's wig, etc).

This has, in the opinion of a numismatist from Newcastle, provided us with another clue towards the expedition's date. The Boots' sketch of the snail at the bottom of page 150 is apparently sufficiently detailed for him to identify the coin on the animal's back as an 1848 British groat or fourpence. Given these creatures' love of decoration it would have seized on the brightest in the box, the most freshly minted. We can therefore deduce that the voyage took place between 1848 and 1855, when Carroll published the first stanza of *Jabberwocky*.

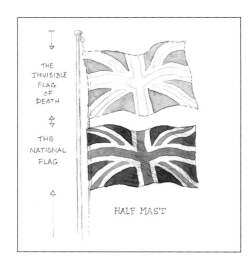

FLAG OF DEATH

BURIAL AT SEA

I cannot leave this last section of the book without commenting on what I consider one of the most poignant of the Boots' drawings, that of the Beaver's funeral. The ship drifts becalmed, steeped in its own sorrowful shadow, its sail drooping. The Union Jack that hangs from the bow at half mast, one flag width below its usual position to allow space for the invisible flag of death, is a fitting tribute, as it was also the official flag of Canada at that time. Similarly, 'God Save The Queen' was

the Canadian national anthem and thus an appropriate memoriam to the Beaver.

There is a bitter twist in the Boots' statement that 'suspicion has fallen on the Butcher'. Despite the Beaver's initial wariness and the Butcher's disdain, it is obvious their relationship had blossomed into one of true friendship and trust. It is an indictment on the nature of mankind that the crew immediately pointed the finger at the poor Butcher when the Beaver disappeared, as is the callous manner in which they passed off the Butcher's suspected suicide a short time later.

As we now know, the man was blameless and probably distraught at the loss of his friend. Of course the Butcher was the only trained killer on board, but there were other suspects. The Bellman, as owner of the Beaver, would have been the beneficiary of any insurance policy the animal might have taken out, and there is a whiff of jealousy as well. The Bonnet-maker may well have coveted a genuine beaver skin for a new hat; and the Broker perhaps had a tenuous motive concerning stocks in Canadian furs. It is even possible that all three colluded in the death of the unfortunate Beaver, in the knowledge that the blame would fall squarely on the shoulders of the Butcher.

Through it all, one senses that the Boojum, stowed away in the ship's coal-hold, would have been immensely enjoying the disquiet it was creating.

THE BELLMAN'S HATBOX AND HAT

The neglected hatbox, left to slide to and fro across the deck during the storm, belonged to the Bellman. Fortunately, given its later function, it was constructed of heavy cardboard and consequently would have been more buoyant than the metal hatboxes prevalent in this period. It has a label, partially obliterated by water and time, which reads *Bingham and Sons, High Street, Oxford. Milliners of discernment.* (In the Bellman's case the reference to discernment is open to doubt.) I have made several attempts to trace this firm, unfortunately to no avail.

The survival of the hat itself, albeit in a dilapidated condition, is a mystery. Why, one might ask, was it not absorbed along with its owner when the Boojum finally struck at the captain on that terrible day? From the Boots' study of the poor Baker as he appeared transfixed to the creature's shell, we can see that the cook was absorbed fully clothed. Surely, given what we suspect of the Boojum's motives—to decorate itself most splendidly with the trappings of power—it would have been at pains to take not only the Bellman but also his bicorne hat, his symbol of authority aboard the ship. Was the hat perhaps blown off in the gale and lost at the crucial instant, only to be found later by the Boots, trapped in the rigging? Or did the Bellman, in a moment of revelation, hurl it from his own head—thus denying the Boojum its prize? It may be of some satisfaction to us all to know that the creature had to make do with the captain's bell alone.

A cameleopard

Origins and species

Nothing has caused more controversy than the biology of the two creatures we know as the Snark and the Boojum. Thanks to the Boots' drawings and notes we have a record of the outward appearance of the animals, but we have no idea about the form of the actual living things that lurk inside these shells.

This gap in our knowledge has led to much speculation on the relationship between the two creatures. Their great difference in size would lead us to be sceptical of the Boots' claim that they are of the same species. Surprisingly, however, there is support for the theory that they are indeed one and the same, the Boojum being a more murderous version of a Snark.

Some academics (who decline to be named) have proposed a transformation similar to metamorphosis, except that in this case the caterpillar does not turn into a butterfly, it becomes a very nasty giant caterpillar. They refer us to ancient times, and the name 'Snark'. Although they cannot find it anywhere in classical texts, they postulate that the word has come into being in much the same way

as 'cameleopard', the archaic portmanteau term for the giraffe, which names an animal that combines the features of two others (humps and spots). They suggest that the Snark is a hybrid of a snail and a shark that, given the right circumstances, can morph into a Boojum. The progression they propose does indeed confirm much of the Boots' theory, and is best explained in the diagram opposite, using illustrations from the Boots' journal.

1. The Snark—half snail, half shark— spawned in the shallows of the sea, is filled with all the ambition of the open ocean but retains the natural timidity of a creature that hides within its shell, and consequently lives in despair born of frustration. The young Snark, brooding in its hollow world, must be content with expressing its hopes and dreams through its shell, which it transforms in any way it can.

2. A few Snarks will venture further, however, and in their wanderings, by accident or design, find themselves an abode of larger proportion and decorative potential. This, our theorists warn, is a

dangerous development. In order to leave one shell for another, the Snark must overcome a little of its natural bashfulness, providing the momentum for the increasing dominance of shark over snail.

3. The Snark that emerges is already a Boojum in all but size, and its hunger for grandeur grows exponentially. It craves—it *needs*—a shell so immense that the creature can no longer carry it on its back. It strives to cover this with all the embellishments and trappings of power it can accumulate.

4. Fatal for the members of our Snark expedition was the Boojum's desire to continue to abandon one shell in favour of another when it sensed an opportunity for advancement. Worse still was its growing appetite for human trophies, which it displayed, much as we might the head of the kudu or the lion, as symbols of domination.

5. No matter what its state or situation, the Snark (or Boojum) cannot defy its marine origins and must return to the sea to procreate. Here it reverts to a

1.

2.

3.

4.

5.

Snark to Boojum

method befitting its inherent shyness and modesty, and we see at last the real reason behind its fondness for the bathing-machine and why it might carry one about. It is not, as Carroll asserts, because the creature thinks the contraption adds to the 'beauty of scenes' but because it provides the privacy essential to facilitate mating. (Perhaps here the Victorian clergyman poet was showing his reticence to dwell on such a delicate matter, and so diverts our attention to the landscape.)

With the emergence of a new generation of small snails gathered at the shoreline, staring yearningly out to sea, the cycle begins again.

The Boots also displays remarkable perception far ahead of his time in his suspicion that it was the intervention of man that created the Boojum. The idea that biological processes might be contaminated by well-meaning natural historians was not considered until

several decades later. If he was right then of course it is likely that Snarks are veritable time-bombs just waiting for the right host (or accidental adventurer) to provide the impetus for the transition to Boojumhood. In fact it is difficult to envisage circumstances where contact between human and Snark would not eventually and inevitably result in the creation of a monster. Something for any future expedition to consider …

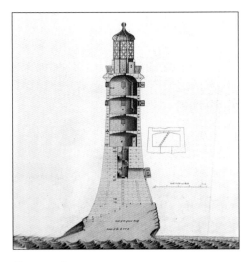

An oyster

Smeaton's tower

Vanishing

The mechanism by which the Boojum dispatches its victims remains a mystery. Some have postulated a theory I personally think lacks credibility. Referring again to the writing of the ancients, they point to Pliny the Elder's *Naturalis Historia*, in particular his entry on the basilisk, a creature the naturalist says can kill with a single glance. We do hear of examples of mesmerism in the animal kingdom, when weasels hunt rabbits, for example, but these instances invariably involve the victim being paralysed with fear, not transfixed 'in the midst of his laughter and glee', as Carroll puts it, writing of the Baker. Also, it seems the victim's body is instantaneously absorbed intact, leaving no sign or mark of what has occurred. As it stands, I think we must leave this puzzle unsolved.

By comparison, the matter of the assimilation of human victims and other objects into the substance of the Boojum's shell would seem straightforward. We have already noted how oysters coat interior irritations with layers of nacre to produce pearls. It seems likely a similar secretion is employed by the Boojum to incorporate a trophy into its exterior.

Home

We know that the Boots had some experience with lighthouses, which could explain his recognition of this particular light as Smeaton's Tower on the treacherous Eddystone Rocks. The metaphor in his notes suggests he was aware that Smeaton modelled his design on an oak tree. Such a thoroughly English image would no doubt have appealed to the Boots. Some say it is remarkable the young artist took the time to dash off this final drawing under the circumstances—but is it really? He seems to have approached this desperate phase of the journey with a coolness far beyond his years.

I consider this the action of a resolute young man resigned to his fate but determined to follow his dreadful tale to the bitter end. I believe the drawing was calculated to provide us with proof of exactly where the expedition reached its shocking finale.

Ambition

The overriding theme of this tragic series of events seems to be *ambition*. The ambition of the Boots that led him to join the expedition; of men to bring the natural world to heel; of the little Snark that produced the Boojum. Perhaps we might even add the ambition that led at least two men to conceal this story from us for so long. Finally we have the vaulting, murderous ambition of the Boojum itself. Once set in motion, in innocence or malevolence, for good or for evil, *ambition* has carried us before it on a pitiable journey.

All we can do is be thankful that the Boots, that brave young man whose true story is now finally revealed, had the courage to run aground the Boojum's insatiable appetite on the jagged rocks of our coast. But for him, that terrible creature and its cohort of Snarks might have colonised our towns and cities, even our beloved Oxford, where this story began. But for him, our great buildings with their columns and spires, their turrets and domes, might be nothing more than homes for gigantic egos, and we plain folk mere pawns and trophies dangling at their whim.

AUTHOR'S NOTE

We do not know if the Boots survived
the expedition. There is no record of him
beyond this point. Perhaps he managed
to swim to shore; perhaps he returned to
Oxford. We can only hope so.

But his notes and drawings *have*
survived, and they present us with a great
mystery. Does his account represent the
true story behind Carroll's great poems
The Hunting of the Snark and *Jabberwocky*,
or is the journal a cruel fraud? Does the
island exist out there still?

I believe the evidence presented here
speaks for itself.

And what of the Boojum? Was it
smashed and destroyed upon the rocks
as our hero hoped, or did it survive? A
disturbing entry was made in the log of
the *Spanish Lady* off the coast of Wales in
1862:

*1900 hrs. Midshipman Thompson reports
sighting a 'muckle Snaile' against the setting
sun, NNW off the port bow. Thrown in the
brig for being the worse for drink.*

Notes picture credits

182 Lewis Carroll, *The Hunting of the Snark* (1st edn), front cover (London: Macmillan and Co., 1876).

183 'You are requested not to speak to the man at the wheel', John Tenniel, *Punch*, 24 August 1854.

184 (left) 'The Railway Juggernaut of 1845', *Cap and Bell: 'Punch's' chronicle of English history in the making, 1841–61*, (London: Macdonald and Co., 1972), 59.

188 (right) 'The Hippopotamus Polka', J. Brandard, cover of composition for piano, c. 1850.

189 (bottom left) 'The Railway Class System', *Cap and Bell: 'Punch's' Chronicle of English History in the Making, 1841–61* (London: Macdonald and Co., 1972), 58.

189 (right) 'The *Comet*', R.H. Thurston, *A History of the Growth of the Steam Engine* (New York: D. Appleton and Co., 1886).

193 (top) 'Eight different styles of beaver hats', Horace T. Martin, W. Drysdale, E. Stanford, *Castorologia, Or, The History and Traditions of the Canadian Beaver: An Exhaustive Monograph* ..., 1892, Bibliothèque nationale du Canada.

194 (bottom) Buckland entering the Kirkdale Cave, W. Conybeare, 1894.

195 (right) A fish-skin helmet, copyright Otago Museum, Dunedin.

197 'Venus's Bathing (Margate). A woman diving off a bathing wagon into the sea', Thomas Rowlandson, 1790.

198 (top left) 'Plesiosaurus battling Temnodontosaurus (Oligostinus)', Thomas Hawkins, *The Book of the Great Sea-Dragons*.

198 (right) Kilsby Tunnel, F.S. Williams, *Our Iron Roads: Their history, construction and social influences* (London: Ingram, Cooke & Co., 1852), 145.

198 (centre) Pears' Soap advertisement, reproduced with kind permission of Unilever from Unilever Archives.

201 Photograph of a thylacine, Tasmanian Archive and Heritage Office, 1930 TAHO:AA193/1/1002.

207 Sea-side amusements, *Cassell's Household Guide, Volume II*, c. 1869.

208 (left) 'A Trump Card(igan)', John Leech, *Punch*, 25 November 1854.

210 (left) 'Queen Victoria of England', Alexander Melville, 1845.

210 (right) 1948 groat, photograph courtesy Steven Mai.

212 Carteret giraffe, Georges-Louis L. Buffon, *L'Histoire Naturelle* (various publishers, 1777–88).

214 'Smeaton's Tower', F. Majdalany, *The Red Rocks of Edison* (London: Longmans, 1959).

ACKNOWLEDGEMENTS

There are many generous individuals, businesses and institutions that have contributed to the making of this book and to all of them I would like to extend my sincere thanks.

Individuals: James Best, Matt Best, Anna Blackman, Andrea Blyth, Pauline Cartwright, Ted Dewan, David Fickling, Commander Bill Gass R.C.N.C. (retired), Emeritus Professor Colin Gibson, Isla Gladstone, Dr Steven Harris, David Hill, Peter Ireland, Chris Jarvis, Lorraine Johnston, Dr Donald Kerr, Andy King, Shirin Khosraviani, Jenny Lister, Peter McLauchlan, Dr Jane Malthus, Dr Timothy Mixter, Dr Haseeb Randhawa, Scott Reeves, Vicki Robson, Dr Shef Rogers, Victoria Shaw, Romilly Smith, Richard Taylor, Joanna Thomas, Professor Lyn Tribble, Timothy Walker, Moira White, Duncan Winning.

Institutions: Ashburton Art Gallery, Alan Dove Photography (Dunedin), Ballast Trust (Glasgow), Bristol Central Library, Bristol Museum and Art Gallery, Brunel Institute, Digi@rt & Design (Port Chalmers), Dunedin Public Library, Hocken Collections (Dunedin), M Shed (Bristol), National Railway Museum (York), Otago Museum, Oxford Museum of Natural History, Oxford University Herbarium, Queensland Museum, Story Museum (Oxford), Tasmanian Archive and Heritage Office, Trinity House (UK), University of Otago Library, University of Oxford Botanic Garden, Victoria and Albert Museum, Weta Workshop. I would also like to thank Creative New Zealand for their support of this project.

Special thanks to Mark Richards, Mark Burstein, Dr Tony Morris and Martyn Baynton for their advice and advocacy. Also to the wonderful Anne Tamati and Sam Cross at Digi@rt in Port Chalmers, Alan Dove for his generous help with photography, and Simone Montgomery and my sister Karen Elliot for their superb sewing and craft skills respectively.

I would also like to thank the fantastic team at Otago University Press—Rachel Scott, Fiona Moffat, Imogen Coxhead, Rhian Gallagher and Glenis Thomas—for their collective expertise and determination to make *SNARK* a book we can be proud of. My gratitude to Fiona in particular, who has toiled over these images with patience and flair.

Lastly and most especially, my thanks to my wife Gillian and my daughters Mhairi and Jess for their constant and unfailing support.

DAVID ELLIOT

www.davidelliot.org

Published by Otago University Press
Level 1, 398 Cumberland Street
Dunedin, New Zealand
university.press@otago.ac.nz
www.otago.ac.nz/press

First published 2016
Original text and illustrations copyright © David Elliot

The moral rights of the author have been asserted

ISBN 978-1-877578-94-6

Published with the assistance of Creative New Zealand

Design/layout: Fiona Moffat

Printed in China through Asia Pacific Offset